CHILL FACTOR

Praise for Vincent McDonnell's writing:

'Sad, frightening, merciless – and unforgettable.'
Graham Greene

'Strong, potent writing.' Antonia Logue

'Vincent McDonnell writes beautifully.' Alice Taylor

Praise for *Out of the Flames*

'Excellent ... uncompromising ... a powerful story.
McDonnell writes with depth and honesty.'
Sunday Business Post

'A thrilling story full of drama and fear.
You won't be able to put the book down.'
Evening Echo

'Combines an exciting story with real and very
topical issues. McDonnell's descriptions are cruelly
graphic and yet told with infinite tenderness.'
Books Ireland

VINCENT McDONNELL's first novel, *The Broken Commandment*, was recommended by Graham Greene and won the GPA First Fiction award in 1989. In February 2004 Vincent won the Francis Mac Manus award, Ireland's most prestigious short story competition, for his story, *Lemon Creams*.

His children's books include: *Out of the Flames, The Boy Who Saved Christmas, The Knock Airport Mystery* and *Children of Stone*. Vincent gives readings and workshops all over Ireland, including at the Listowel Writers' Week and the Wexford Arts Festival. He has served as Writer in Residence for counties Limerick and Cork. Born in Mayo, Vincent now lives in County Cork with his wife and son.

CHILL FACTOR

VINCENT McDONNELL

THE O'BRIEN PRESS
DUBLIN

First published 2004 by The O'Brien Press Ltd,
20 Victoria Road, Dublin 6, Ireland.
Tel: +353 1 4923333; Fax: +353 1 4922777
E-mail: books@obrien.ie
Website: www.obrien.ie

ISBN: 0-86278-888-9

British Library Cataloguing-in-Publication Data
McDonnell, Vincent, 1951-
Chill factor
1.Children's stories
2.Suspense fiction
I.Title
823.9'14[J]

1 2 3 4 5 6
04 05 06 07 08

The O'Brien Press receives
assistance from

Typesetting, editing, layout and design: The O'Brien Press Ltd
Printing: Cox & Wyman Ltd

For Joan MacKernan,
with gratitude for your friendship and support.

ONE

When his father had not returned by 4am, Sean Gunne knew that something was wrong. He had slept fitfully since his father had phoned him shortly after dashing from the house to attend a traffic accident. Now fully awake and apprehensive, Sean played that call over in his mind.

'Sean! Sean!' Denis Gunne's voice had sounded tense, his urgency cutting through background noises which Sean couldn't make out. 'It's Dad. I think I've been–' There was what sounded like a gasp. Then the line went dead.

Sean had immediately dialled his father's mobile. It rang a number of times before it was answered. 'Yes?' It was a man's voice, but not his dad. There was a hint of an American accent.

'I was just talking to my father,' Sean said. 'We got cut off. Can I speak to him?'

'Sorry,' the man said. 'He's attending to the injured. I'll get him to call you as soon as he can.' The line went dead for a second time.

That was over two hours ago, and there had been no word since. Sean sat up and reached for the phone and dialled his father's mobile again. A recorded message told him the phone was out of range or switched off. He hung up and, with an increasing sense of foreboding, got out of bed and crossed to the window.

Orchard Road was quiet, bathed in the soft glow of the streetlights. Below his window, the driveway was empty. In the next-door garden, Sean caught a movement from the corner of his eye. A cat was slinking across the lawn. It stopped and

7

crouched by the hedge. Suddenly it sprang. Sean shivered and felt his body go cold.

No sound carried to his ears. But in his imagination he heard the stricken screech of the cat's prey – probably a fieldmouse. He sensed the creature's terror and felt its pain as if the cat's razor-sharp claws were tearing his own flesh. Sickened, he closed his eyes, overwhelmed by an ever-increasing feeling of apprehension.

There was no one to share his fears with and he felt acutely alone. It was a sensation he'd experienced often since his parents had split up. Now more than ever, he wished he was back at their old home. His grandfather slept just down the hall, but he was suffering from the onset of Alzheimer's and was easily confused if he was alarmed or upset. Sean knew he could not burden him with his worries.

+   +   +

'Don't go, Dad,' he had pleaded earlier, made uneasy by the emergency call that had woken him. He had heard his father speaking on the phone in the bedroom next door and then the sounds of him getting dressed.

Emergency calls, even late at night, were a normal part of a GP's life. But this one, because of recent events, had alarmed Sean. So much so that he had got out of bed and gone to his father's room.

'There's been an accident,' his father had explained. 'Down at the roundabout. A child's been thrown through the windscreen.'

'Why didn't they call an ambulance?' Sean asked.

'They did,' his father said, lacing up his shoes. 'But one of the drivers is local and he called me. The child is badly hurt and I can be there before the ambulance. It might make all the difference.' He straightened up and reached out to ruffle Sean's unruly hair. 'So, back to bed with you,' he added. 'No point in us both missing a night's sleep.'

With that, he had dashed from the room and bounded down the stairs. Sean had followed him out to the landing. His father retrieved his emergency bag from under the stairs. At the front door, he turned to glance up at Sean. 'Don't go, Dad,' Sean begged. 'Let the ambulance deal with it.'

'There's a little girl hurt,' his father said, a note of reprimand in his voice. 'I have to go.' Then he was gone. Sean heard the slam of the car door and the engine start up. He ran back to the window in his room in time to see the car accelerating down the street, its exhaust belching white vapour. He watched until it disappeared from sight, somewhat shamed by his selfish behaviour. He wanted his father to think the best of him, but tonight he had shown a side his father wouldn't admire.

A cold breeze from the hall sent him scurrying back to bed where he snuggled down beneath the duvet. He dozed restlessly, his dreams filled with dark shadowy figures. Now, standing by the window for the second time that night, he felt those shadowy figures near and fear replaced his shame.

There was something wrong. His father was in danger. The lurking menace that had been encroaching on their lives for months had become real.

It had all started four months ago when an addict had come to the surgery demanding that Doctor Gunne prescribe drugs for him. He'd thrust a fistful of soiled euro notes at the doctor and had become abusive when his demand was refused. As he left, he claimed that it was common knowledge that Denis Gunne was crooked.

Since then many other young men and women had called on a similar quest. They were all alike, with pinched faces and running noses and eyes filled with desperation that turned to naked hatred when they too were refused. One openly made threats, and that night the windscreen and side windows of Denis Gunne's car were smashed.

One morning, over a week ago, the police came. They were in the house for over an hour. When they left, his father had taken Sean aside. 'You have a right to know what is happening,' he said. 'The police are accusing me of selling prescriptions to addicts and supplying them with drugs. But that's something I would never do. You must know that, Sean.'

Of course he knew – had always known that his father was the most decent man alive. 'I know you wouldn't do anything wrong, Dad,' he said vehemently. 'And surely the police can't have any evidence against you?'

His father's face grew dark with worry. 'I'm afraid they have,' he said quietly. 'A number of addicts who've been arrested have claimed that I supplied them with drugs for money. Then, when my car was vandalised – or so I thought at the time – a prescription pad was stolen from the glove compartment. I kept it for emergencies and didn't realise at first that it was missing. I had a lot on my mind then, as you know ...'

He stopped for a moment, his face contorted with anxiety. 'Someone's been forging my signature on the prescriptions and selling them to addicts. The police have a number of them. They think they have a case against me.'

'But ... but why, Dad? Why would someone do this to you? Who would do it?'

'I don't know,' his father said. 'But whoever it is, and for whatever reason, they want to destroy me.'

Sean couldn't imagine who could hate his father that much. His dad had no enemies. But false rumours didn't just materialise out of thin air. And whoever had stolen the prescription pad and forged his father's signature hadn't done it solely for money. They had to have had another motive. But what could it be?

Sean took deep breaths and tried to rein in his racing thoughts. Then, coming to a decision, he turned abruptly from the window and dressed hurriedly. On the landing he listened at the door of his grandfather's room. The old man was snoring and Sean knew he wouldn't wake for hours yet. Satisfied, he ran lightly down the stairs and slipped out of the house.

Above the roofs, the sky was suffused with the first pink tinges of dawn. But Sean had no eye for the morning's beauty. He hurried along the street and turned right at the end onto the main road. The roundabout was a quarter of a mile further on. When he reached the spot, it was deserted. Sean walked all around it, seeking evidence of an accident. But all he found were a few shards of dirty red glass, and they looked as if they had been on the road for some time.

He knew that the accident could have been cleared and that his father might have gone to the hospital with the victim. But there were no skidmarks, no remnants of shattered glass that would surely have flown in all directions after the impact, no sign of blood having been washed off the road. There had been no accident. It had been a ruse to lure his father from the house. Whoever was trying to destroy him had become desperate and more reckless. Whatever their motive, it seemed to have taken on a new urgency.

Alarmed, Sean retraced his footsteps. He had almost reached Orchard Road when a car approached from behind. Fearful, he turned to look as a police car pulled alongside him. The garda in the passenger seat had his window rolled down.

'What are you doing out at this hour?' he asked, an edge to his voice.

'Was there an accident tonight?' Sean asked. 'At the round-about?'

The garda shook his head and glanced at his colleague. 'Not as far as I know,' he said. 'What's your name, son?'

'Sean Gunne.'

'Do you live around here?'

'Just there,' Sean said, pointing towards Orchard Road.

The man's eyes narrowed and he glanced again at his colleague. 'You Doctor Gunne's son?' he asked.

Sean nodded. 'Ah,' the garda said. 'And where are you coming from?'

Sean recounted the night's events. The garda took a book from his pocket and made some notes. Then he used his radio to inquire if there had been an accident. As he clicked off the radio mike, he looked puzzled.

'No accident's been reported,' he said. 'Your father must have used it as an excuse to go out. No doubt he's got his reasons. Now, I'd be getting along home, if I were you. It's not safe out alone at this hour of the morning.'

Sean wanted to shout at the garda that his father would not lie to him. But if there had been no accident, then *someone* had been lying. And where was his father now?

Sean turned away without a word and walked back home. He went into the kitchen and sat at the table. Agonisingly slowly, the clock ticked the seconds and minutes away. From the garden came the sound of birdsong, and as the sun rose, the room emerged from the shadows. From upstairs came the faint sound of a radio; it was the 7.30am alarm.

His father was not coming back. Something had happened to him. He had been lured from the house, almost certainly by whoever had spread the rumours about him. Sean had never felt so isolated. He missed being with his mother and Liam, missed the closeness of the happy family they had once been. How could he tell Liam that his beloved father was missing – that 'Doctor Dolittle', as Liam called him – had gone out into the night and not returned?

Sean got up and picked up the phone. He dialled his home number, hoping that Liam would not answer. 'Hello.' It was his mother's voice

Sean explained the night's events and his mother laughed. He hated that laugh, just as he hated the cold, impersonal voice she had acquired lately. 'Oh, I wouldn't worry,' she said. 'He knows how to take care of himself. He's just gone out. I've heard rumours of ... well never mind.'

'But he wouldn't lie to me,' Sean said, aware as he spoke that he was beginning to have his doubts. But if his father *had* lied to him, he must have had a good reason. Had he gone to meet whoever it was had spread the rumours?

'I have to get Liam ready and go to work.' His mother's voice cut across his thoughts. 'I'll talk to you later.'

'But what if he doesn't come back?'

'He'll be back,' she said.

'Bye, Mom,' he said. 'Say hi to Liam. But don't mention anything to him about Dad.'

He hung up before she could reply. He switched on the electric kettle; his grandfather would be up soon and looking for his breakfast.

As Sean began to ready the table for breakfast, he searched his mind for any reason why someone would want to take his dad. Maybe it went back to when he had been a research scientist?

After qualifying as a doctor, Denis Gunne had moved into the field of genetic research, and had established an international reputation for his work. But he began to have serious misgivings about the direction genetics was taking and gave it all up to retrain as a GP. Sean knew that genetics was an important and very lucrative field. A new discovery could mean billions to a company. His father had often spoken of industrial espionage and how research scientists were frequently bribed to divulge their findings to rival companies. Maybe he knew something from his former work that made him valuable to these people?

As he took the milk from the fridge his eye caught the photograph that sat on top. It had been taken on the day his father started his GP practice. In the picture he was clearly happy. Sean was smiling too, and Liam, seated in his wheelchair, had a grin on his face that threatened to engulf his ears. Beatrice Gunne stood a little apart from the group. There was a forced smile on her face, but her eyes were cold.

Sean turned away. There were sounds of movement from upstairs; his grandfather was getting up. Sean glanced at the clock. It was 8am. Standing in the kitchen, he closed his eyes. What was he going to do?

TWO

For two days, Sergei Bukanov, with the help of Denis Gunne, had been planning his escape. Now he was ready and about to tackle the most difficult part – getting out of the castle undetected and down to the shore of the island.

He picked up the plastic shopping bag in which he had concealed his spare tracksuit and trainers. Inside was a second plastic bag, its opening heat-sealed with a soldering iron so that it was waterproof. Another smaller sealed bag contained the precious computer disk.

He rolled up the outer bag, and then tied it tightly with nylon cord, leaving sufficient length to encircle his waist. Tucking it beneath his arm, he surveyed the room that had been his home for weeks. It was little more than a cell beneath the castle. There was a narrow bed, a wardrobe and locker; a desk littered with papers and books; a chair.

'Mr Silvermann is not a patient man,' Costello had said on Bukanov's first day here, laughing in that sinister way Bukanov now knew so well. 'He expects results within six months. If your work is not satisfactory or you break any of the rules, we have somewhere special where you can think about what you have done wrong. And I promise you, you won't like it!'

Bukanov shivered at the memory. When he had refused to work he had found out what Costello's 'special place' was: a dank, airless space in the very bowels of the castle, with barely enough room to move, and not a single shaft of light to illumine the pitch darkness. It was known as the 'black hole'. He had been so overwhelmed by the experience that if it hadn't been for Denis Gunne, who had persuaded him to co-operate, he might now be insane or even dead.

'If we want to try to escape and stop whatever project Silvermann is working on here, then we must pretend to co-operate,' Gunne had said, speaking in halting French because Bukanov did not speak English. 'I know your family is dead, but mine is alive. I want to see my sons again.'

Since he arrived on the island over a week ago, Gunne had spoken continually of his family, the hurt of his marriage break-up etched on his face. It had mirrored Bukanov's memories of his own family, killed in Chechnya by a Russian missile. He had been pulled from the rubble of their apartment building forty hours after the blast, unaware that his wife and children were dead. It had been dark beneath the rubble, and bitterly cold, with the stench of death all around. But it was the fear of slow suffocation that had tortured him and continued to haunt his nightmares.

Confined in the black hole, he had relived his entombment and knew that madness was close. But Gunne had saved him – it was Gunne who had first brought up the subject of escape. 'You could make it to the mainland and raise the alarm,' he said excitedly when Bukanov mentioned that he had once been a champion swimmer.

'It was a long time ago,' the forty-three-year-old Bukanov protested. 'I was young and fit then.'

'You're still fit,' Gunne said. 'You could make it. And wouldn't it be better to drown in the attempt than to remain here? They can never let either of us go. You know that.'

Put like that, it made sense. But the main problem, as Bukanov saw it, was not swimming the eight kilometres to the mainland, but getting out of the castle in the first place. They were held underground, in what were originally the castle dungeons, now greatly enlarged. The only exits were two staircases, both blocked off by electronically operated steel gates. One stairs gave access to the ground floor, the other to the top floor of the tower. A code-operated lift served both floors.

On Bukanov's first day here, Costello had taken great pleasure in displaying his security measures. The castle was alarmed and under constant video surveillance. All doors were controlled by electronic locks and opened only when the correct code was punched in. An underwater cable from the mainland supplied electrical power and there was a back-up generator to maintain the security measures and radio communications in the event of a power cut.

Outside, surveillance cameras covered the only exit, and four Rottweillers prowled the security fence. Costello had offered to let Bukanov see them in action. Suppressing a shiver, Bukanov declined.

'Even if you escape from the castle, there is no way of reaching the mainland,' Costello had boasted. 'The cruiser that is tied up at the jetty requires a coded card to start it. The only way out of here,' he added, laughing, 'is to swim for it.'

Now Bukanov was to attempt just that.

At the door of his cell he peered out. The single surveillance camera covering the main corridor was fixed above the archway that gave access to the mainframe computer room, which also housed two giant intake fans. It was Gunne who had pointed out that the camera would only pick up someone walking upright. If you crouched down, you couldn't be seen.

The neon-lit corridor was deserted. At this time of night, the other scientists – Brandt, Dubrek and Stewart – were asleep. Only Gunne knew of the escape attempt. The others could not be trusted.

For most of the time, the scientists were allowed to move about freely within the confines of the underground area. But every day, often without warning, they would suddenly be ordered back to their cells. On these occasions Bukanov would hear the lift descending, and the door to the strongroom, situated beside the lift, would open with a hiss of compressed air.

No one knew what lay behind the steel door. Stewart said that one day he had glimpsed a man in a wheelchair emerge from the room, accompanied by another man. Both were dressed as if for a skiing trip. Stewart claimed that the man in the wheelchair had been crying. But no one really believed him on that.

Crouching down as low as possible, Bukanov crept out into the corridor, through the archway and into the computer room. There, his interest lay not in the computer but in one of the huge intake fans. That was where he hoped to find a way to freedom.

'This castle was once owned by a reclusive pop star,' Denis Gunne had told him when they'd first spoken of escape. 'One night he was attacked by a crazed fan who apparently rowed across to the island and managed to get into the castle through an underground passage at the lowest level. I heard that it was a tunnel used by smugglers in the nineteenth century. If the passage still exists, it could be the escape route we need.'

Bukanov had been sceptical of the story, suspecting that it was just part of local legend. But the next time he was alone in the computer room he examined the rock walls and the fan housings. He noticed a discoloration on the stone floor beneath one of the fans. The discoloration was caused by stone dust from when they had cut the rock to form a recess for the fan housing. He checked the floor beneath the second fan; it was clean. That could only mean one thing: they hadn't had to cut the rock *because a hole already existed.*

Did this prove Denis Gunne's story? Was this the entrance to the underground passage leading to the sea? Soon he would find out.

The grey steel cabinets that housed the mainframe computer were ranged at the rear of the room, opposite the entrance. A fuse box was attached to the wall nearby. Bukanov had checked it previously and discovered that each fan had its own separate circuit breaker, clearly marked. It was a simple matter now to open the box and flick off the switch that controlled the second fan.

The only other equipment in the room was a coffee machine and a mineral water dispenser. The coffee machine sat on a steel locker that contained supplies of coffee, sugar and long-life milk. Two days earlier, Bukanov had taken an unopened packet of coffee, emptied the contents down the toilet and hidden a screwdriver and pliers in the empty packet. Carefully folding the top of the resealable packet, he placed it at the very back of the cabinet where it wouldn't be discovered.

Now he retrieved the tools and began to work on the fan housing, using the screwdriver to remove the outer louvred grill. He could see the recess into which the housing was fitted. The edges were uneven and he could make out chisel marks on the stone. The opening had been cut by hand and it was obvious that the work had been carried out a long time ago.

Greatly encouraged, Bukanov pressed on. His next task was to unscrew the housing from its retaining clamps. The screwdriver was much too small for the job and at times he despaired of succeeding. But eventually the housing came free.

The fan and its housing were too heavy to lift, so he eased the housing out until it was balanced on the edge of the stone. Then he let gravity complete the task. As if in slow motion, the housing toppled onto the floor with a resounding crash.

Bukanov held his breath. Even above the roar of the other fan, the noise seemed loud enough to be heard all over the castle. Tensed, he waited for the guards to come pounding towards him. But no one came.

Breathing a sigh of relief, he stared into the recess. Immediately his heart sank. It wasn't much more than one metre deep. On the top edge he could see an opening for the air inlet pipe. But that offered no escape route.

Bukanov knew he was in serious trouble. If he didn't make it out, Costello would send him to the black hole, a fate worse than death as far as he was concerned. Taking deep breaths to calm his thumping heart, Bukanov closed his eyes and concentrated. Why would someone, using a hammer and chisel, cut a recess in solid rock? It could possibly have been used for storing wine, but the space was very small. So, was it an attempt to reach an underground passage leading to the sea, and had the attempt failed? But a metre could hardly be considered a determined effort. And why had the aperture been formed so neatly if the attempt had failed?

That didn't make sense. Surely the logical thing to do would have been to make sure there was access to the passageway first and then shape the aperture? If a way out hadn't been found, there was little point in tidying up what had been done. But it *had* been tidied up. Did that mean that a way out had been found? So why was the tunnel blocked?

The truth dawned suddenly and Bukanov cursed himself for being a fool. The tunnel had to be blocked for the fan to operate properly. If it was left open, the fan would have sucked in stale air from the tunnel and not fresh air from the pipe leading to the surface.

He leaned in and tapped the back of the recess with his knuckles. It sounded hollow, which meant that what was blocking the tunnel certainly wasn't stone or brick. Encouraged by his discovery, Bukanov lifted himself, feet first, into the space. Gripping the housing brackets with his hands, he kicked at the rear wall. He felt it yield. On the third kick his foot penetrated the wall. It was plasterboard. He continued his assault until he had an opening large enough to crawl through.

He clambered back out and stared into the cavity. Beyond the now jagged plasterboard there was darkness. Bukanov shivered. He wished he had a torch. There was nothing for it now but to go forward into that darkness.

In other circumstances he knew that the fear of being trapped underground in the dark would have stopped him. But he had no choice: if it wasn't the tunnel then it would be the black hole, and Costello was ruthless enough to let him rot in there.

Taking long, deep breaths to calm his nerves, he picked up his plastic bundle and clambered head first into the recess. He wriggled his way through the opening and glanced back. He could still see light and it helped ease his feeling of panic.

He crawled on, aware that the tunnel was dipping and curving to his left. When he looked back, the light was now little more than a glow. Then it was gone and he was in utter darkness.

Terror gripped him. He was back in Chechnya again, his eyes and mouth filled with blinding, choking dust. He felt paralysed, unable to move. Every fibre in his body urged him to scream for help. It was illogical, for he would not be heard. But this panic had little to do with logic.

Slowly the paralysis eased and he crawled on unsteadily, his knees trembling. The tunnel held its shape, obviously man-made. Which meant that it had been cut for a purpose, almost certainly as an exit to the outside world.

It was all the encouragement Bukanov needed. He redoubled his efforts and soon broke into a larger space. Feeling about with his hands, Bukanov found that the walls and floors were uneven, jagged in places. This was a naturally-formed opening, not manmade.

As he progressed, the tunnel, which sloped downwards, got larger still. Soon he was able to get to this feet and walk, hunched over. Shortly afterwards he could straighten up and he sensed that he was in some sort of a cave. He felt his way along the walls and found an exit into another, larger tunnel. He moved cautiously on, still going downwards, becoming aware of a faint glow up ahead. Relieved and overjoyed, he broke into a trot. The light grew stronger and now for the first time he could hear the roar of the sea. He reached the mouth of the tunnel and breathed in the ozone-tinged air. The night seemed bright after the utter darkness and he wanted to breathe in the light too. He moved around the pile of rocks that would have concealed the exit from the eye of a casual observer, and saw the sea spread out beneath him like a flat sheet of lead.

In the distance he saw the lights of Oldport. They seemed a long way away, and now that he had made it this far, his thoughts turned to what lay ahead of him. It was at least eight kilometres to the mainland – a daunting swim. In his youth it would have been a formality, but he was no longer young or fit, despite what Denis Gunne thought. But he had come this far and there was no going back.

He stripped off his tracksuit and trainers. Bundling them up, he hid them behind a rock. Dressed now only in shorts, he tied the plastic bag about his waist and scrambled down to the water's edge.About twenty metres above him, the castle loomed, its dark bulk outlined against the backdrop of the high-powered security lights. He turned back to the sea and waded into the water. It was bitterly cold. He should have taken precautions – rubbed fat or grease on his body as a barrier – but it was too late for regrets.

The water lapped at his knees. It was a perfect night for swimming, there was hardly a puff of wind and the sea was so calm. But the waters out there could still be treacherous.

He took a deep breath and thrust forward. He plunged his head under the water and tasted the salt on his tongue. Then, shaking the excess water from his hair, he settled into a smooth breaststroke, aiming for the beckoning lights ahead.

He did not look back.

THREE

Three hours after Bukanov entered the water, a red warning light blinked on a console in the control centre at the castle. The guard on duty, dozing in his chair, was unaware of it.

Night duty was tedious. Nothing ever happened or seemed likely to happen. The scientists were secured underground, with no means of escape. In any event, they, along with many of Mr Silvermann's employees, were either wanted by the law or had some other reason for keeping a low profile, so the island was as much their sanctuary as it was a prison.

Money was another inducement that kept the inhabitants of Fair Island content. They were well paid and assured of substantial bonuses when the project here was completed. They had been promised new identities and access to any country in the world. To Hawk Silvermann, a multi-billionaire, money was no object.

And even if someone did escape from the castle, there was little chance of getting off the island. It was a long way to the mainland across treacherous water.

The sleek, seagoing cruiser, 'Spirit of Abraham', moored at the jetty on the western side of the island, was well secured. There was a fast motorboat and a dinghy, but they were kept at the castle and had to be transported to the sea on trailers when required. Mr Silvermann's helicopter was also well secured.

In the control centre a buzzer sounded, alerting the guard. He started in surprise and rubbed sleep from his eyes. Then, glancing at the dials on the main console, he sighed with relief. It was only a minor matter: part of the electrical system had failed.

He leaned forward and tapped the keyboard in front of him. Within seconds he had located the problem. Number two fan in the computer room had cut out, causing the temperature to rise above the set threshold.

The security guard stared at the monitor, undecided what to do. His orders were to alert Costello if an alarm sounded. But you never knew with Costello; if he was woken up for such a minor problem, he could fly into one of his rages. And the guard certainly didn't want that. He decided to wait.

Over the next hour, the temperature increased. At two degrees above the permitted threshold, the guard reached for the telephone.

'Get Donlon onto it right away,' Costello snarled. 'Why should he be allowed to sleep when I've been woken up? Now sort it out and don't disturb me again.'

Ten minutes later the telephone beside Costello's bed beeped insistently. He snatched the receiver from its cradle, his face changing as he took in what the maintenance engineer, Donlon, was saying.

'Alert the guards. Check the cells – now!' he shouted. 'Make sure the strongroom is secure.'

As he gave his orders, he was already scanning the strongroom monitoring systems on his own computer screen. They were normal and he sighed with relief. If the strongroom's security or cooling system had been compromised, then his life wouldn't be worth a bent nickel.

Dressing quickly, he made his way to the control centre.

'The strongroom is secure,' he was informed. 'But Bukanov's missing. It looks like he escaped through a tunnel behind number two fan.'

Seething with rage, Costello tried to calm himself. The unthinkable had occurred. Now it was imperative that the situation be contained. Then Hawk would have to be informed. Costello wasn't looking forward to that.

Costello briefed his security team. 'I want the castle and the island thoroughly searched,' he said. 'Check 'Spirit of Abraham'. We must stop Bukanov getting off the island. Go ... go!'

As his men hurried off, Costello prepared for the daunting task of breaking the news to Hawk Silvermann. He rehearsed what he would say as he took the lift to Hawk's quarters at the top of the square tower that was part of the original castle. This area was out of bounds except to Costello and to Hawk's personal assistant, a powerfully built deaf-mute named Quigly. The man was in his Hawk's debt and would kill without question if his boss's life was threatened.

Costello got out of the lift at the top of the tower and walked along the stone hallway. Heavy oak doors opened off the corridor, giving access to the various rooms. The door to Quigly's room stood open. He had been alerted as soon as Costello summoned the lift. Unable to hear a warning buzzer, Quigly wore a special electronic device on his wrist that vibrated when anyone entered the tower via the lift or the stairs.

Using basic sign language, Costello conveyed to Quigly that he needed to speak urgently with Hawk. Quigly nodded, his pockmarked face expressionless. Indicating to Costello to stay where he was, he walked slowly to Hawk's bedroom. Moments later he returned and beckoned Costello to follow him.

Hawk's inner sanctum was a grim affair; the walls were painted black, and black blinds covered the narrow windows. On the floor, polished black slate shone in the dim light. There was a large desk with a computer on it and beside it, Hawk's powered wheelchair.

A great black iron bedstead dominated the middle of the room. In the centre of the bed lay a large man, his face small and deathly pale against the black pillows. His head was shaved and glistened in the light. But it was his eyes that were his most remarkable feature. They glinted like diamond shards despite the gloom and gave the impression that they were twinkling. It was only close up that one realised that they were hard, cold eyes, bereft of any emotion.

Costello felt the eyes on him as he crossed the room and stood beside the bed. 'Yes?' The man in the bed spoke. The voice was low, hardly more than a whisper, yet there could be no mistaking the menace in that single word.

'We have an emergency,' Costello said. 'Sergei Bukanov has escaped. My men are searching for him now.' He waited for the tirade of abuse and threats, but none came.

'Is he still on the island?' Hawk asked.

'Almost certainly,' Costello said firmly. 'Bukanov cannot get off the island.'

'Why escape then?'

Costello swallowed. Behind him he heard a rustle of clothing as Quigly shifted his position. Costello knew that, despite his knowledge of martial arts and his long years of violence on the streets of his native Bronx in New York, he was no match for the man. Quigly could snap his neck like a twig.

But he was safe for now, he reasoned. Hawk needed him, and Hawk was a pragmatic man. He would do nothing rash. But it was no guarantee that he wouldn't act later.

'Bukanov's desperate,' Costello said, trying to answer Hawk's question. 'He's been depressed, as you know. He's simply panicked. He's not thinking rationally.'

'Maybe,' Hawk said. 'Now give me the details.'

Costello did so. For a moment there was silence. 'Check out everything we know about him,' Hawk ordered. 'Bukanov's no fool; I don't agree with your analysis. He would not make an escape attempt simply in the hope that chance might throw up an opportunity of getting off the island. He must have had reason to believe that he could reach the mainland.'

'Very well.' Costello turned to leave.

'Wait,' Hawk commanded. 'Do it here.'

Costello nodded and crossed to the computer terminal. As the screen flickered to life, his walkie-talkie beeped. He unclipped it from his belt. 'Yes?' he answered, his voice hopeful.

'Corridan here. The boats are secure. The 'Spirit's' tied up at the jetty. We're searching her now.'

'Good.' Costello was relieved. 'Continue the search. I want the fugitive back within the hour.' He re-clipped the radio to his belt. 'He hasn't taken a boat,' he said, turning to Hawk. 'So he's still on the island. We'll have him shortly.'

There was no response and he turned back to the computer screen. He tapped the keyboard and called up all the information held on Bukanov. The material had been put together by Hawk's researchers when they had targeted Bukanov as a possible recruit for the project.

He scanned quickly through the data. There were details of Bukanov's work as a geneticist at Moscow University, until he lost his position with the fall of the Soviet Union. Then there was the death of his family in Grozny during the Russian-Chechen war. His time with a Chechen rebel group and his desertion were noted. There was a gap then, until he turned up in Britain seeking political asylum. His request was rejected and an order made to deport him. It was then that Hawk Silvermann had offered him sanctuary on Fair Island in return for his expertise, and promised him a new identity when the project was completed.

Costello scrolled up and down the screen, pausing here and there to re-read a section. Then he stopped dead, his mouth agape, a chill coursing through his body. There it was, listed under 'other achievements'. Bukanov had been a champion swimmer, just missing out on Olympic glory through injury.

Costello's skin felt clammy. If Bukanov managed to reach the mainland and raised the alarm ... he shivered. Costello was wanted in Texas for murder. If he were extradited and convicted it would mean execution by lethal injection.

He swung about, his whole body tensed like a drawn bow. Quigly moved between him and the bed. 'Bukanov was a champion swimmer,' Costello said, trying to keep his voice level. 'That's how he intends getting off the island.'

'He must be stopped,' Hawk said flatly. 'See to it. I'll have Quigly put the emergency evacuation plan on standby. We must be prepared for any eventuality. We will speak about the security lapse later.'

'Of course,' Costello said. 'Now if you'll excuse me.' He nodded to Hawk, sidestepped Quigly, and ran from the room, hoping that he wasn't already too late.

Down in the control centre a report awaited him. A tracksuit and trainers had been found hidden at the exit from the tunnel, more proof, if Costello required it, that Bukanov was attempting to swim to the mainland. 'He's in the sea,' Costello shouted. 'Let's go find him. There's a bonus for the man who brings him back. Alive or dead – it doesn't matter which.'

FOUR

Bukanov had hoped to make it to Oldport under cover of darkness, but his age and lack of fitness took its toll and dawn was lightening the sky by the time he neared the shore. The currents too had conspired against him, dragging him off course and making the journey that little bit longer. His arms felt like lead and he began to experience the twinges in his leg muscles that signalled the onset of cramp. But he couldn't afford to stop now. He had no idea how long he had been in the water and his absence would be discovered at the regular 7am inspection. With a last-ditch effort, he pressed forward, willing the lights nearer and nearer, until he felt the scrape of shingle on his knees

He crawled the last few metres out of the water and collapsed onto the sand, gulping air into his lungs. Then he pushed himself to his feet and looked back. Fair Island was spotlighted by the rising sun, the castle hardly more than a dark speck at this distance. The sea glittered as if sprinkled with shards of glass.

Suddenly Bukanov went rigid. There was something out there, between the shore and the island. Shading his eyes against the glare from the water, he squinted into the distance. The shape resolved itself into a boat – and it was heading towards him!

Panic and fear engulfed him. He looked around for shelter. About a hundred metres from him stood a row of high sand dunes. If he could make it there unobserved he might have a chance. But if he could see the boat, then they could see him, especially if they were using binoculars.

He began to run for the dunes, crouching low to present as small a target as possible. His fatigue dropped from him as fear imbued him with new energy. He sprinted the last few strides and rolled himself over the top of the dune. He lay there for a few moments, winded. Then, cautiously, he edged forward and raised his head.

There were two boats out there now. The one he had first seen – a speedboat – had come in closer. Further along the shore was a larger craft. As he watched, it seemed to him that they were operating in a pincer movement, closing in on a point they had obviously decided was where he was most likely to come ashore. Hope coursed through him. They hadn't seen him! And, more importantly, they hadn't allowed for the effect of the currents that had borne him further north.

Encouraged, he untied the nylon cord from around his waist and carefully unrolled the plastic carrier bag. He removed the heat-sealed bag, tore it open and took out the spare tracksuit and sneakers. Dressing quickly, he thrust the small bag containing the precious disk deep into his pocket, and then buried the wet shorts and torn carrier bag.

Before setting off, he stole a quick glance out to sea. The bigger boat was making for Oldport. Two men stood in the cockpit of the speedboat, which was heading for a point about two hundred metres from his present position. Even from this distance he could tell that one of the men was Costello. He had a pair of binoculars clamped to his eyes, scanning the dunes.

Fear gripped Bukanov. How had they discovered his escape so quickly? But there was no time to think about that now. He had to get on. He ducked down, then began to head forward, keeping under cover of the dunes. Where the sand gave way to grass, a row of mobile homes marked the entrance to a small caravan park. Some children were already out playing. He was tempted to knock on one of the doors and ask for help, but the language barrier prevented him.

He broke into a slow jog, cutting through the park, glad of the cover provided by the caravans. The road exited by a golf course, deserted at this hour. Soon he came to the first houses and a row of shops. Most premises were still closed. He had memorised the sign for a garda station that Denis Gunne had drawn for him; he searched anxiously for it. There was a junction up ahead with numerous signs. He was relieved to see that one of them pointed to a garda station. He turned left, in the direction indicated, and stopped dead. Coming towards him was one of the guards from the island.

They saw each other simultaneously. The guard began to walk towards Bukanov. He raised a mobile phone to his mouth and spoke into it urgently. Bukanov retreated, his heart beating wildly. The guard would be summoning help, telling the others of Bukanov's position. How long did he have before they closed in on him? Up ahead, he saw a complex of buildings enclosed by a high stone wall over which he could see red signal lights. A railway station!

From around the corner at the end of the street a man came into view. It was another of the castle security men. On seeing Bukanov he began to quicken his step. Trapped, Bukanov looked around frantically for a way out. Just ahead of him there was a break in the stone wall – a pedestrian access to the station?

He darted in and found himself at the far end of the station. Tall black iron railings separated him from the track. The place seemed deserted. Suddenly a horn sounded in the distance, signalling the approach of a train. He raced past the unmanned booking office and pushed open the swing gate to the platforms. There was no sign of railway staff or of any other passengers, but someone had left a red rucksack on one of the wooden seats that bordered the platform.

Bukanov did a quick calculation. Even if the train arrived right now and he got on, what chance was there of escaping? Slim? No, none. His pursuers knew where he was; they would simply board the train and recapture him. But if he could prevent them from getting the disk, then his swim would not have been in vain.

His mind made up, he ran up to the rucksack, pulling the bag with the disk from his pocket as he went. He tore open the bag and removed the disk, stuffing the torn bag back in his pocket. The plastic clips on the flap of the rucksack proved difficult to undo. He squeezed a section of the clip with his right hand and then tried to pull the other section away from it with his left hand. But he couldn't grasp it properly while he held the disk.

Feverishly he tried to force the sections apart, but they wouldn't budge. Then he noticed the three zipped pockets in the front of the rucksack, just below the flap. He yanked one of the zips and it opened easily. He slipped the disk into the pocket and zipped it closed. As he did so, he heard footsteps and glanced up. A girl had come out of the waiting room. When she saw him crouched over the rucksack, she ran at him, shouting.

Bukanov began to speak quickly, explaining that he had put something in her rucksack and that she should take to the police. When he saw the look of incomprehension on the girl's face he realised that he had spoken in Russian. How could he make her understand? Maybe she spoke French? Pointing at the rucksack, he started again ... then a movement caught his eye. Costello stood at the end of the platform.

Bukanov swung round and found one of the security guards blocking off the swing gate. A third man – the one who had followed him – was at the main entrance to the station. There was no way out. The platform vibrated beneath his feet as the train entered the station. If he could get to the other side of the tracks and put the train between himself and his pursuers, he might just make it. It was his only chance, and anything was better than recapture and the terrors that awaited him in the castle.

The engine loomed towards him. Bukanov hesitated, gathering courage. He took a deep breath and stepped forward. Then he leapt out into empty space ...

FIVE

Jackie Howley had no qualms about leaving her baggage on the platform; Oldport station was always deserted on Sunday mornings. And anyway, who would want to take an old rucksack? So she was astounded, on emerging from the waiting room with her can of Coke, to see a man crouched over the bag.

Her initial reaction was one of anger, and, without thinking, she ran towards him. He, on the other hand, seemed unable to move. As he stared up at her, she had a good look at his face. It was taut with fear and something else – desperation maybe?

'What do you think you're doing?' she demanded.

He jabbered in a language she didn't understand, waving his hands about wildly. He then glanced around and, whimpering like a frightened puppy, leapt to his feet.

From the corner of her eye she noticed that another man had come onto the platform, right at the very end. It was his presence that had caused the crouching man to whimper. Then she noted a second man at the other end of the platform. There was something unnerving about them, and as they began to walk forward, she had the impression that they were stalking prey.

Frightened, Jackie drew back into the doorway of the waiting room. The sun was warm, but she felt chilled. She wished there were others about, but only the signalman was on duty at this hour and he was too far away to help.

The train was entering the station. The two men were still advancing. The thief, for that's how she thought of him, seemed like a cornered animal.

If those two men hadn't arrived on the scene, what might have happened to her, Jackie wondered? Would he have attacked her? Or would he simply have run away? And what had he been doing with her rucksack anyway? If he intended robbing her, why hadn't he just grabbed it and run?

The engine had reached the far end of the platform. Jackie caught the terror-stricken eyes of the thief. To her surprise, they seemed to be pleading for help.

The advancing men quickened their pace. There was a sudden desperate resolve on the thief's face. A split second before he leaped onto the track in front of the train, Jackie knew what he intended. She tried to scream a warning, but the cry caught in her throat.

The train whistle blasted urgently. She heard the screech of wheels as the emergency brake was applied. She turned away, her stomach heaving. Above the din, she distinctly heard the sound made by her drink can as it fell from her powerless hands and Coke foamed at her feet. Mercifully, she sensed rather than heard the sickening crunch as the engine struck him. She held onto the doorjamb, fighting nausea. As if it were happening in another world, she heard doors opening and shouts above the rumble of the engine. There were running footsteps. Somewhere a child cried.

A hand touched her shoulder and she turned around. 'Are you all right?' a woman asked anxiously. Jackie nodded. The nausea receded and she became aware of her surroundings. A knot of passengers had already gathered by the engine. She glanced both ways along the platform, searching for the two men she had seen earlier. They had disappeared.

There was a mixture of horror and excitement on the summer air. Down on the rails a man lay, crushed and broken, yet above the train she saw birds flitting across the sky as though everything was normal. She wanted to go and check if he was dead, but she couldn't bear to look just now.

He had been so terrified that he had chosen to leap in front of the train rather than face those two men. Who were they that they could inspire such fear, and where were they now?

Feeling her legs weak beneath her, Jackie stumbled into the waiting room and flopped down on one of the wooden benches. The single window was grimed over and she couldn't see the activity outside. It was some small mercy.

Passengers came into the waiting room. Some stared at her, but she ignored them. She watched them get drinks from the machine, talking excitedly. Two women came in and sat near Jackie. Though they were whispering, she could hear what they said. They were talking about the man on the tracks. Only one word registered with her – dead!

In the distance she heard the sound of approaching sirens.

SIX

Costello took the lift to the tower to make his report and was shown into the darkened bedroom by Quigly. He crossed to the bedside where Hawk lay breathing heavily. 'Bukanov is dead,' Costello began and launched into his explanations before Hawk could respond. As Costello spoke, Hawk's breathing grew more laboured.

He completed the report, using both fact and conjecture to paint a picture of what he thought had occurred. During all this time Hawk did not utter a word. Now Costello waited, fear making him sweat. At a nod from Hawk, Quigly could kill him as easily as swatting a fly.

'This is disastrous,' Hawk said starkly. 'The police may already be on their way. You must prepare to evacuate.'

'Everything is ready,' Costello said.

'Very well. Now I must visit ...' His voice trailed off.

Costello nodded and withdrew. He made his way down to the control centre to await developments. Normally when Hawk visited the strongroom, the scientists would be sent back to their cells. But today they were already confined there.

When the lift began its descent, Costello made his way to the dungeons via the stairs, opening the steel gate by punching in the code on the keypad beside it. As Hawk emerged from the lift, Costello stood waiting. Hawk and Quigly both wore Gore-tex suits. They had scarves wrapped about their lower faces so that only their eyes were visible.

Quigly punched in the code for the strongroom door. The pneumatically controlled door swung open with a hiss of compressed air. Clouds of white vapour billowed out and Costello felt the air temperature drop suddenly. He stepped back. He was not allowed enter.

Hawk manoeuvred his chair through the door. Quigly followed. The door swung shut, cutting off the vapour and the chill.

Hawk remained in the room for twelve minutes, much longer than usual. When he emerged, his body was shuddering. Costello always felt discomfited at this show of emotion, but Quigly's face remained expressionless.

Hawk guided the chair to the lift and he and Quigly ascended to the tower. There Hawk would spend hours alone in his bedroom. He would remain sitting in the chair or sometimes would lie on the bed, staring into the darkness.

As the lift ascended, Costello ordered that the scientists be summoned to the library. Although he was pretty certain that Gunne had helped Bukanov escape, it might not be easy to prove. But he was going to make the situation plain to all of them. He would not tolerate another breach of security.

The scientists were seated around the conference table when Costello entered. Brandt, as supervisor, occupied a seat at the head of the table. Stewart and Dubrek sat on one side. Denis Gunne sat alone on the other. Just inside the door stood Corridan, Costello's second-in-command, his arms folded. A holster beneath his jacket held a 9mm Luger.

Costello's sharp eyes swept the room as if he were a bird of prey. Slowly he shifted his gaze from man to man, dwelling for a moment on each, seeming to peer into their very souls. 'Bukanov is dead.' Costello's voice was cold and menacing. 'He tried to escape and has paid for his foolishness with his life. He has endangered the project and also your lives and freedom. We had offered him asylum here and a new life when the project was completed. But he has thrown that in our faces.'

He stopped, as if waiting for a response. But they all appeared too shocked to speak. 'I hope that none of you here knew of this stupidity or colluded in it. But if you should know of anyone who did, then speak now. That person is endangering all of us. Does anyone have anything to say?'

'What happened to Sergei?' It was Denis Gunne who spoke.

'He jumped in front of a train.' Costello voice was cold, detached.

'At Oldport? So he reached the mainland?' Gunne sounded both sad and resigned.

'It is not your concern,' Costello said. 'Your only concern is to obtain results. When you do, we can all leave here.'

'If we knew more about the project and what it is we are trying to achieve,' Brandt said, 'then we might make more progress. All the laboratories, except for the one on genetic research, are fully functioning now, yet my colleagues are working in the dark. It is not a very satisfactory situation.'

'I will speak to Mr Silvermann,' Costello said. 'It's his decision as to what you should or shouldn't know. That's all. Now, go back to your quarters until further notice. Not you, Gunne,' he added. 'You wait here.'

The others left, along with Corridan. Gunne stood up and faced Costello, the animosity between the two men palpable. 'I know you helped Bukanov escape,' Costello said. 'But you only succeeded in killing him.'

'No.' Denis Gunne's voice was as cold as Costello's. 'I didn't kill him; I gave him a chance for freedom. *You* killed him.'

He took a step towards Costello.

'One day you will have to answer for his death, as well as for whatever horrific experiment your boss intends us to carry out here. I will personally see to it.'

Costello laughed, but there was no humour in the sound. 'Don't threaten me,' he said. 'You're the one who has lost.'

'No,' Gunne said. 'You might have killed Sergei and recovered the disk, but–' He stopped abruptly. Costello had jerked as if subjected to an electric shock. For a moment there was complete silence.

'What disk?' Costello demanded, a nerve twitching in his cheek.

Gunne could have cursed himself for a fool. Why hadn't he kept his mouth shut about the disk? But it was too late to reprimand himself for that now.

'The disk explaining our situation here,' he went on quietly, aware that he had nothing to gain by lying. 'As you know, Bukanov didn't speak English. He wouldn't have been able to explain without an interpreter. So I put it all on a CD. He had it with him.' He could hear Costello trying to control his panicked breathing.

'You didn't find it!' Gunne said triumphantly. 'So Sergei didn't die in vain. His death will bring an end to all of this. The information on that disk will free us and put you and Silvermann behind bars for a very long time.'

Costello's face screwed up in rage and fear. He opened his mouth to speak, but as he did so a siren began to wail. It started on a low note, becoming louder and shriller until the castle walls themselves seemed to be screaming.

Costello reacted instantly. He stepped into the corridor and grabbed one of the internal telephones fitted at intervals along the walls. 'Yes?' he barked. Moments later the alarm ceased. Costello hung up and grabbed his walkie-talkie.

'Emergency!' Costello spoke urgently into the mouthpiece. 'Police are on their way. Ten minutes to evacuation. Scientists to be confined in the bunker. Everyone to his station immediately.'

A guard appeared within moments. He crossed the book-lined library, and as he did so, a motor began to hum at the end of the room. A section of a bookcase slid back to reveal an immense steel door. The guard punched a code into the keypad on the wall and the door slowly swung inwards.

Just then the other three scientists were herded into the room, protesting loudly. 'In, in,' Costello ordered, pointing towards the opening. 'Bukanov's stupidity has brought the police. I'm sure you don't want to renew acquaintance with them.'

The protests ceased and the men complied with Costello's order. Only Gunne remained. At a sign from Costello, one of the guards grabbed Gunne by the shoulders and propelled him through the doorway.

Inside was a large room, lit by fluorescent tubes. A line of tiered bunk beds took up one wall. There was a kitchen area and a scattering of couches and armchairs arranged around a flat screen television.

As the steel door began to close, Costello ran back up to the control centre to oversee the evacuation plan. He was certain the police had found the CD and were acting on the information it contained. This was the end of everything.

He checked that all was under control. Hawk and Quigly were standing by for evacuation. Two men flanked the strongroom door, under instructions to move its contents to the helicopter when given the order. If this became necessary, the policemen would be held prisoner while Hawk and Quigly and the strongroom's precious cargo were flown to a secret location.

From there they would be taken back to Texas where, no doubt, Hawk would continue to pursue his obsession. Costello had no intention of being left behind, and if Hawk tried to prevent him from coming with them, Costello had decided to kill both him and Quigly and force the helicopter pilot to fly him to safety.

One of the internal phones rang, disturbing his thoughts. Costello picked it up. 'The police are on their way up to the castle,' a voice told him. 'Just two: it looks like a sergeant and a garda, both in uniform.'

Costello heaved a sigh of relief. They mustn't have found the CD. If they had, they would have come in force, not sent two unarmed uniformed men. His conclusion was confirmed when the police arrived and explained that they were investigating Bukanov's death.

'We have reason to believe that he may have been an asylum seeker who came ashore from a boat this morning,' the sergeant said. 'Did you, or any of your people here, see anything suspicious?'

'No.' Costello shook his head.

'And no one's missing from the island?'

'No.' Again Costello shook his head. 'Everyone is accounted for.'

The sergeant nodded. 'Well, if you should see anything suspicious – anything at all – you'll let us know?'

'Of course,' Costello said. 'This man who was killed,' he went on. 'He had no identification on him, then?'

'Nothing,' the sergeant said.

Costello could hardly believe his luck. There was no mention of a CD, no awkward questions, no demand for a search. The police were simply carrying out routine inquiries. They had no evidence linking Bukanov with the island.

'If we can help in anyway,' Costello said, shaking hands with the policemen as they left, 'then don't hesitate to call me.' He watched them depart, then hurried up to the tower to report to

Hawk, deciding not to mention the missing CD. Hopefully, Hawk would never have to know about it.

Silvermann listened to the report, his face as inscrutable as Quigly's. When Costello finished, there was silence for a moment, disturbed only by Hawk's laboured breathing. 'You have been fortunate,' he said eventually. 'This time. But I won't tolerate any further breaches of security. You understand?'

'Absolutely.' Costello spoke the single word with complete conviction.

'I want the scientists to resume work immediately,' Hawk went on. 'From now on they will work seven days a week. I must see some progress soon.'

'Brandt suggests that now that the laboratories are fully functioning, except for Gunne's, he should be allowed tell the other scientists what it is they are working on,' Costello said. 'He claims that things will go better if they have a clear idea of what it is you are hoping to achieve. I told him I would speak to you about it.'

'I'll think about it,' Hawk said. 'I'll let you know what I have decided.' He raised a hand. Costello was dismissed.

After releasing the complaining scientists from their confinement and ordering them to get back to work immediately, Costello retreated to his own quarters and sat in thought for some time. Coming to a decision, he summoned Corridan and ordered an inventory of Gunne's re-writable CDs.

After thirty minutes, Corridan came back to report that a single CD was missing. Costello was baffled. If Bukanov had taken a CD with him, and the police hadn't found it, then where was it? Could Bukanov have lost it in the sea? Or dropped it? Maybe he had hidden it somewhere?

There was, of course, the possibility that Gunne was bluffing. Deciding that he couldn't afford to take that chance,

Costello ordered a search of the island and sent two men to the mainland, with instructions to retrace the route Bukanov had taken from the time he was seen by the first security guard. Costello reasoned that the scientist would have tried to hide the CD only after he knew they were on to him. And, assuming that it did in fact exist, Costello was determined to find and destroy it.

SEVEN

On Monday morning Jackie Howley was at work in her father's Dublin office. His receptionist was ill and he had asked Jackie to cover for her. 'It's best for you to be occupied, Jackie,' he'd said. 'It'll take your mind off that terrible event yesterday.'

But nothing could take her mind off it. Over and over again she saw that terror-stricken face pleading with her. He had tried to rob her and yet had been begging for her help. It didn't make sense.

She had watched the television news the previous night, but there was very little new information. Although the victim had not been identified, gardaí claimed that he was a foreigner. They gave no explanation as to how they knew this.

The morning papers had covered the story. Jackie's own account was there, along with her picture. Though not exact in every detail, the report was close enough to what had occurred. It mentioned the two men who had been seen on the platform, and added that the gardaí were anxious that the men come forward so that they could be eliminated from their enquiries. Apparently, Jackie was not the only one to have seen them; the train driver had also spotted them.

When interviewed by the gardaí, Jackie had played down the fact that she thought the man had been trying to rob her. 'Nothing's missing from my rucksack,' she had told them 'There was nothing of value in it – just clothes and books and CDs. I had my Walkman and mobile phone and money with me.'

The gardaí seemed sceptical that the man might have been frightened for his life. Or, more specifically, frightened of the two men who'd been on the platform. 'He tried to get away from them, didn't he?' Jackie had pointed out a little testily. 'He did jump in front of the train and was killed.'

When she read the newspaper reports, she realised why the gardaí had doubted her story. They seemed to think the man might have been deranged. Apart from the fact that a sane person would hardly have thrown himself under a train, several witnesses had heard him mumble the words 'Doctor Dolittle' before he died.

Jackie didn't believe the man was mad. Terrified out of his wits, yes, but not insane. And that claim about 'Doctor Dolittle' was just nonsense. Why, he didn't even speak English! He'd obviously been trying to say something in his own language, and it had been picked up wrongly.

Jackie completed some typing and filing and was about to go to lunch when a boy walked into the office. Dressed in a dark tracksuit, he was fair-haired, lightly built and and wore a worried expression. He seemed surprised to see someone as young as himself behind the reception desk, but did his best to conceal this fact.

'Yes?' Jackie said. 'Can I help you?'

Suddenly a look of recognition crossed the boy's face and he became animated. 'You're Jackie, the girl who was at Oldport station yesterday. When that man jumped in front of the train?'

Jackie nodded. The boy took a step towards her. She could see a gleam of excitement in his blue eyes. He put his hands on the desk and leaned towards her. 'Did ... did he speak to you?' he demanded. 'What did he say?'

'Nothing,' she said. 'I mean, he spoke, but I couldn't understand him. It ... it sounded foreign.'

The boy seemed frustrated at her answer. 'But he *did* say something,' he insisted. 'I read it in the paper. About Doctor Dolittle ...' His voice broke as he spoke the name. 'I have to know. It's important.'

She was about to tell him not to be ridiculous, but he was obviously so serious that she stopped herself. 'He didn't say that to me,' she said quietly. 'It was someone else who claimed he mumbled Doctor Dolittle. When he spoke to me it was in a foreign language. I didn't understand a word of it.'

His disappointment was obvious. He blinked, as if there was something in his eye, and snuffled. 'Thanks, anyway,' he said, and turned to leave.

Jackie's curiosity was aroused. What interest did this boy have in the incident yesterday, and why did he want to know if the dead man had spoken to her? 'Wait,' she said. 'Why did you come here? '

'I ... I don't know,' he shrugged. 'It was stupid, I suppose. I'm sorry I bothered you.'

'Wait,' she said again as he made to leave. 'How did you know who I was?'

'I saw your picture on the paper,' he said.

'And how did you know where to find me?'

'It said on the paper that your father was a security

consultant, so I looked up his name and address in the Golden Pages. But I didn't expect that you would be here.'

'But why did you want to speak to me?'

He hesitated. 'It's to do with my father,' he said. 'He's been missing for over a week. I thought you might be able to help me find him.'

'Haven't you been to the gardaí?' she asked. 'Surely they find missing persons.'

'They don't believe he's missing,' he said quietly. 'They think he's ... well, that he's gone away. Then when that man mentioned Doctor Dolittle, I thought it might be a clue.'

'Oh.' Jackie tried to hide her scepticism. So this boy thought his father was Doctor Dolittle?

'I knew you wouldn't understand,' he said, suddenly bitter. 'Why should you when no one else does?'

'But Doctor Dolittle,' she said. 'I mean ... well there's no such person. He's just a character in a film.'

'I *know* that,' he said. 'But that's my father's nickname. His real name is Denis Gunne but my brother Liam nicknamed him Doctor Dolittle. So when I read what that man said ...'

'But what could he have to do with your father?' Jackie said.

'I don't know,' he said. 'I think that man knew something about my father. It's just such a strange thing for him to say, especially if he was a foreigner. It's ... it's a feeling I have. I can't explain it better.'

'It's OK,' she said. 'I think I understand.'

'So you don't think I'm being foolish?'

'No,' she said quietly. 'Not after what I saw yesterday. There were two men who terrified that poor man. He was so scared that he jumped in front of the train rather than let them catch him. I'd like to know why that was.' She hesitated. 'Look,' she added. 'I'm just going to lunch. You can join me if you like and tell me about your father. OK?'

'OK,' he nodded. 'But let me pay?'

'Right,' she laughed. 'It can be my fee!'

They found an empty corner in a nearby McDonald's and retreated there with their Big Macs and fries and milk shakes. On the way from the office, Jackie had learned that his name was Sean and that he lived with his father and grandfather. He didn't mention his mother and she wondered if, like her own mother, she was dead.

As they ate, Sean explained about his father's disappearance. Jackie stared at him in disbelief. If her father were missing for even a day, she'd be frantic. 'But someone just can't disappear like that,' she said. 'And who made the emergency call? Haven't they been traced?'

'The call was made from a pay-as-you-go mobile,' Sean said. 'It couldn't be traced.'

'But what do the gardaí say?' Jackie asked. 'What have they found out?'

Sean took a deep breath and began to speak. In a rush he told her about the addicts coming to the surgery and the accusations made against his father. As he spoke, his face became suffused with anger. He put down his burger and clenched his fists.

'I'm sorry,' he said. 'I ... I get so mad. My dad is the most honest man you could ever meet. He would never do these things. You ... you have to believe me.'

His earnestness convinced her. 'I believe you,' she said quietly. 'So tell me the rest.'

'Dad's car was found at the ferry terminal. The gardaí concluded that he had gone to England. But he would never run away. He would never leave myself or Liam or Granddad. And even if he had gone away, he'd have contacted us since.'

'The gardaí think that I know where he is and that we are in touch. But it's not true. Then when I read what that man said yesterday I thought it might be a coded message from my father – that he was trying to tell us that he was all right. Or else was asking for help. You see, it was such a strange thing to say.'

Jackie remained silent. It *was* a strange thing to say. And it must have been very important for the man to waste his dying breath trying to get whatever message it contained across.

She stared at Sean, trying to imagine his pain. He was so straight and open that she believed him utterly when he said his father wasn't mixed up with drugs. But why would someone be making false accusations against him?

'Would *your* father go away and not contact you?' Sean asked now, his words breaking into her thoughts.

'No,' she said. 'He wouldn't.'

'Mine wouldn't either,' he said. 'So the only explanation is that he's unable to make contact – that someone is preventing him from doing so.'

Or else he's dead, Jackie thought, and then thrust the thought away. 'But why would someone abduct your father?' she asked. 'And where is he? If he can't get in touch, then he must be a prisoner.'

'I know,' Sean said. 'It's a real mystery. He had nothing of value and very little money, so that wouldn't be a reason for taking him. In fact, my mother was always complaining about how little money he earned as a GP. It takes time to build up a practice and it was just coming good when this happened.'

'It was one of the reasons he and Mum split up,' he went on, his voice low, tinged with sadness. 'When Dad qualified as a doctor he was offered a job doing research with a multinational pharmaceutical company. He was very good at it, the pay was great and he also got shares in the company. He travelled all over the world, something my mother loved.'

'But he became disillusioned with the work. He had gone into medicine to help people, and he felt the company he worked for were only interested in money. He had real worries about the ethics of some of the things they were doing, so he gave it all up to become a GP. He sold his shares to keep the family going while he was setting up his practice. Shortly afterwards the company floated on the stock exchange. His shares, if he had kept them, would have made us rich. My mother was bitter about that too and it led to even more rows. Eventually Dad moved out to live with his father. I usually stay there with them when there's no school.'

'So he was a research scientist, then,' Jackie said.

'In genetics,' Sean said. 'He was an expert in his field.'

'Would he have had valuable information?' Jackie wondered aloud. 'There's a lot of money in pharmaceuticals. Could someone have abducted him to get that information? A rival company, maybe?'

'It's possible,' Sean said. 'But it would have to have been for something big; it's a serious offence to kidnap someone.'

Jackie nodded. That made sense. But a man simply didn't vanish into thin air. So who had taken him and where had they taken him? That was the mystery.

'Now you see why I was so interested in that man yesterday,' Sean went on. 'And in what he said.'

'Yes,' Jackie said. She hesitated a moment. 'I could talk to my dad about it,' she continued. 'He used to be a garda and he's originally from Oldport. I'll ask him what he thinks. So, if you call again tomorrow, I'll let you know what he says. You'd better let me have your phone number, and email if you've got it.'

They exchanged phone numbers and email addresses. 'Thanks,' Sean said. 'I appreciate what you're doing.'

'That's all right,' Jackie said. 'Now I'd better get back. I'll talk to you tomorrow.'

They said goodbye and parted. He seemed nice, Jackie thought as she returned to the office. It must be terrible for him to have his father disappear and to be carrying all that worry around.

She wanted to help Sean, but there was very little she could do. But she could ask her father for his opinion on the mystery. It would be a start, and at the moment anything would be better than nothing.

EIGHT

On that same Monday morning, Costello was summoned to Hawk Silvermann's study. Hawk sat in his powered chair behind the walnut desk, his hands resting on the polished surface. He didn't ask Costello to sit.

'Bukanov's escape and death has placed my project in jeopardy,' Hawk said. 'I hold you personally responsible. When Bukanov is identified, the police will learn that he was a geneticist. That may focus their attention on us. And if by chance they or a nosy journalist should happen to link Bukanov with the other missing scientists ...'

He stared at Costello, giving the latter time to contemplate what he was implying.

'So it is essential right now that we do not draw further

attention to Fair Island,' Hawk continued. 'As you know, I've been negotiating the sale of part of my business empire. A member of that consortium offered to buy Fair Island.

'At the time I refused to consider selling. As a family, we were happiest here. And when I first dreamed of my project, I was on Fair Island in the dream. It was here I saw my project succeed. But it was just a dream, nothing more, and it was a mistake to come to a place where I have to work outside the law just on the basis of a dream.

'The location has become a liability so I'm now considering selling it. I will be contacting the prospective buyer today. If the sale is agreed, I will take my project to a country where such research is not illegal. Then I can hire the best scientists and work openly without fear of the law. But all that will take time. Meanwhile I want to see more advances made here. I've decided that Brandt should give his colleagues some limited information about the project. Have Brandt sent up so I can discuss this with him.

'I am relying on you to see that things start moving, especially with Gunne – we need his cooperation. If you succeed, then you will have earned yourself a very large bonus when the project comes to fruition. I presume I can leave the matter in your hands?'

'Certainly,' Costello said, his eyes glinting with greed. Things were working out better than expected. He hated this place with a passion, considering himself as much a prisoner here as Gunne, so the prospect of moving to another location was more than welcome.

'Tell the scientists that the sooner I achieve my goal, the sooner they gain their freedom and the substantial financial package I've promised. That should be enough incentive for them to work more diligently,' Hawk went on. 'Even Gunne will be more willing to co-operate.'

'But you can't free him,' Costello said. 'If you do, he'll go to the police and you'll go to prison. We all will.'

'I think not,' Hawk said. 'When I have fulfilled my dream, I will have the means of buying Gunne's silence. I can offer him something he wants more than life itself.'

Hawk closed his eyes. He seemed to drift away. Costello stared at him, made aware again of how out of touch with reality Hawk really was. If he thought he could buy Gunne's silence, then he was mad. And if Hawk went to prison, Costello would join him there. That was a prospect Costello intended avoiding at all costs.

Brandt, Stewart and Dubrek had good reason to remain silent and to disappear with their reward. Gunne, on the other hand, would not stay silent or disappear no matter what Hawk thought. But there were other means of ensuring that he did. A fatal accident could be easily arranged. Whatever happened, Costello intended protecting his own skin.

Hawk seemed to come out of his reverie.

'Send Brandt to see me,' he ordered. 'And carry out a complete review of security.'

Costello withdrew. As he left the tower, Quigly hovered by the lift. He stared at Costello as the lift doors closed, latent menace in every taut muscle. It seemed as if Quigly could read minds, and Costello shivered.

As he descended, Costello wondered what the reaction of the scientists would be when they were told of Hawk's plan. Costello himself had been shocked when Hawk accidentally revealed what his real goal was. But scientists were a breed apart, cold fish, if the truth were known. They were interested only in their research and not in its possible consequences. And anyway, Hawk didn't intend telling them the whole truth about his project. That would come later, and by then there would be nothing they could do about it, even if they wanted to.

Back in his room, Costello arranged for Brandt to see Hawk, and then began to consider his own problems. The most pressing one right now was the missing CD. There was always a possibility that Bukanov had lost it during the swim, but Costello thought this unlikely. So where was it?

An intense search of the island and a more discreet search on the mainland had come up blank. How had Bukanov got rid of it? Costello had read the newspaper reports, hoping for a clue, but found none. He picked up the papers again and reread the articles; there was nothing there that he didn't know already. He looked at the photographs: the beach at Oldport, the railway station; pictures of the girl whom Bukanov had tried to rob ... Costello paused, his hand about to turn the page. Something in one of those photographs had caught his eye. He searched through the papers until he found the one he was looking for. It was a picture of Jackie Howley, taken as she left Oldport Garda Station. A portable CD player hung around her neck.

Costello's heart began to thump loudly. Carefully he reread what the girl had said. 'I went into the waiting room and got a Coke from the machine. When I came back out, I saw the man crouched beside my rucksack.'

Costello sat quietly, considering the conclusions that had been drawn from the girl's statement. In the circumstances it had seemed logical to suppose that the man had been intent on robbing her. But what would Bukanov be trying to steal from her?

Costello threw the papers aside and summoned Corridan. 'Find out everything you can about this girl, Jackie Howley,' he said, pointing to her picture. 'I want a full report within the next four hours.'

Denis Gunne lay on his bed in his cell, desperately trying to come to terms with recent events. First, there was the devastating news of Sergei's death. Costello had shown him the newspaper reports so that he could be in no doubt of its veracity. Bukanov had made it to the mainland, only to die like a dog in the end.

Then Brandt had called a conference, and informed the scientists of Hawk Silvermann's goal: to use stem cells from embryos to help him walk again. In the next few days Brandt would allocate each scientist an area of research in their field of expertise. Gunne had already concluded that Silvermann was deranged. Only now did he realise the extent of that madness. And as he did so, he came to realise what it meant for him.

It was a death sentence. Despite the promise of freedom and money conveyed through Brandt, Silvermann could not allow him to live once his goal was achieved. By abducting him, he had placed himself outside the law. And where did Silvermann intend getting the embryos? That, too, would have to be done illegally. So if he released him, Denis Gunne reasoned, then Silvermann was sentencing himself to a long term of imprisonment. Why would he do that?

As a scientist, Gunne knew that the billionaire's dream could be fulfilled. When that happened, Gunne would be of no further use and would be disposed of. In fact, why not have them all killed? Why leave any loose ends?

Gunne had tried to impress this on Dubrek and Stewart, but failed. They believed Silvermann's promise that they would be given their freedom along with a sizeable financial reward.

'We can't go to the police,' Dubrek explained. 'If we do, then we endanger our own freedom. We are all fugitives in one way or another. Silvermann is aware of this. He knows he has no reason to fear us.'

'And what about Sergei?' Gunne asked. 'Who pays for his death?'

'Bukanov came because he saw this place as a sanctuary, just like myself and Stewart and Brandt. No one forced him,' Dubrek said. 'He made an agreement, as we have, but he broke it. It was his decision to try to escape. You encouraged him. So if anyone's to blame for his death, it's you.'

The words, cold and blunt, pierced Gunne like a knife. He turned away and went back to his cell. Since then he had lain on his bed, feeling utterly alone. He missed his family. What if he died here a prisoner, never seeing his sons again?

He came to a decision. He would not co-operate with the project unless Silvermann agreed to contact Sean and Liam and inform them that their father was alive. Silvermann would have no choice but to agree to this demand. Right now he couldn't afford to go looking for a new geneticist and risk drawing attention to himself or Fair Island – not with Bukanov lying dead in the morgue just eight kilometres away.

Gunne rose and pressed the communication button in his cell. Costello came within a few minutes. 'I want to speak to Hawk Silvermann,' Gunne said.

'No one sees Mr Silvermann,' Costello said.

Gunne walked past Costello and went along to his section of the laboratory. He picked up his chair and, before Costello could intervene, began to smash the equipment.

It took Costello and two guards to subdue him. As the guards held him, his arms pinioned to his sides, Costello stared at him. 'You're a fool,' he said. 'You think you can defy me? Well, you'll have some time in the black hole to consider your situation. After that, if you still refuse to co-operate, I'll have you taken out and thrown into the sea – with a rock tied to your body.'

Gunne returned the stare, determined not to be intimidated. 'You need me,' he said. 'Your boss needs me. Where will he find another geneticist? So he won't let you kill me.'

Costello laughed. 'Mr Silvermann is moving his project to a country where the laws are more liberal,' he said. 'Somewhere he can work openly and recruit openly. It will be easy to find a dozen geneticists then. After all, he pays well. When that happens he won't need you.'

Costello gloated at Gunne's shocked face. 'Take him away,' he ordered.

The guards marched Gunne down to the black hole. When the door closed and he found himself in darkness, Gunne sat down and hugged his knees to his chest. This was the beginning of the end.

He would never agree to co-operate with Silvermann, even though it meant certain death. After what Costello had told him, he didn't for one moment doubt that Hawk would let Costello kill him.

He put his face in his hands and took deep breaths to calm himself. But he was close to despair. They had broken and killed his friend Sergei. Now they would break him. This place would not only be his prison, but also his tomb.

NINE

'Of course I know about it,' Stephen Howley told Jackie when she asked him at breakfast about the disappearance of Denis Gunne. 'It caused quite a scandal – a respectable GP who lived a double life.'

'What do you mean, a double life?' Jackie asked.

'I heard that he was mixed up with some very dangerous characters: drug addicts and pushers mostly. He supplied them with drugs and illegal prescriptions.'

'But why would he do that?' Jackie asked.

'Why does anyone do anything?' her father said. 'It's usually for money. Although I suppose he could have been black-mailed. Probably both.'

Jackie remained silent. They were sitting at the kitchen table, the daily papers strewn about them. They carried further reports of the accident at Oldport, but there was nothing new. The gardaí had not identified the dead man. He'd had neither papers nor money on him.

The mystery man, as the papers referred to him, had been seen jogging through the caravan park on the morning of his death. But there was no evidence as to where he had come from. Inquiries had not identified anyone matching his description living in Oldport, or holidaying there.

The gardaí had confirmed that he was a foreigner, and much speculation centred on the possibility that he was an illegal immigrant who had been put ashore from a ship. People who'd seen him at the caravan park remembered that his hair had been wet. But that, ultimately, proved nothing.

'Could you get some information for me, Dad?' Jackie asked.

'I suppose,' her father shrugged. 'What exactly do you want to know?'

Jackie took a deep breath and told her father of Sean Gunne's visit to the office. As a former garda, her father had learned to listen, and he heard her out without interruption. Afterwards he sat quietly toying with a teaspoon.

'It's a strange story,' he said eventually. 'But the evidence for this man having anything to do with the missing Doctor Gunne – well it's certainly flimsy. We don't even know if the victim did use the words 'Doctor Dolittle'. Remember, he was dying at the time.'

'But supposing he *did* say it,' Jackie persisted.

'OK,' Stephen Howley said. 'There can be no harm in making inquiries, and no time like the present. I still have contacts in the gardaí in Oldport. You clear up and I'll make a phone call.'

While she cleared the table, Jackie heard her father speaking on the phone in his study. He spent a long time on the call and was looking thoughtful when he returned to the kitchen.

'The gardaí have made more progress than they've admitted to the press,' he said. 'Firstly, they know the identity of the dead man. He was a Russian named Sergei Bukanov. He was a scientist – a geneticist apparently – and worked at Moscow University before the break up of the Soviet Union. His wife was a Chechen and she, along with their children, were killed by Russian troops during a missile attack in Grozny.'

'Seeking vengeance, Bukanov joined an extremist Chechen rebel group. They wore a distinctive tattoo on their arm – that's how he was identified so quickly. But it seems that he couldn't accept the atrocities perpetrated by his group. So he deserted and fled to Britain, seeking asylum. He was refused and was going to be deported when he simply disappeared. That was two months ago. No one had seen or heard of him again until he turned up at Oldport on Sunday.'

'But what was he doing in Oldport?' Jackie said. 'And how did he get there? He was really terrified, Dad. I saw him. Who-ever those two men were, he jumped in front of the train rather than face them.'

'We don't know that for sure,' her father said. 'Those men may be perfectly innocent.'

'You wouldn't say that if you had been there,' Jackie insisted. 'Maybe ... maybe they were from that rebel group, and that's why they haven't come forward.'

'Maybe,' Stephen said doubtfully. 'We simply don't know. But it's still possible that they had nothing to do with Bukanov's death.'

'No!' Jackie said. 'That's something I am certain of. They were involved in some way.'

'OK,' her father agreed. 'Let's accept that. But we are still no nearer to finding out who they were or why Bukanov was terri-fied of them. Or indeed what he was doing in Oldport in the first place. It's a mystery, whichever way you look at it.'

Jackie had to accept this. 'Did you find out anything else, Dad?' she asked.

'Not really. Only that the gardaí think Bukanov came ashore from a ship that morning. That he was fleeing Britain to evade deportation. Forensic tests show that he was recently in contact with salt water. He also had a small heat-sealed bag in his pocket. It had been torn open and was empty. The gardaí think it must have contained his papers and money. So he'd either lost them or hidden them.'

'So that's that,' he continued. 'When you consider it all, it seems most likely that he was an illegal immigrant, and that he came ashore from a boat that morning.'

'Or maybe he came from Fair Island?'

Stephen Howley laughed. 'I admire your persistence,' he said. 'But I'm afraid you're on the wrong track. Fair Island was the first place the gardaí checked. No one was missing from there. And there's no way Bukanov could have swum from there. So I think we can rule out Fair Island. Anyway, why would they lie about it?'

'They'd have to lie if he were a prisoner,' Jackie said.

Her father laughed again. 'You have a vivid imagination too, I'm afraid. Why would Bukanov be a prisoner on Fair Island?'

'I don't know,' Jackie said. 'It's just that Granddad Howley told me that Max Silvermann, the American who owns it, was a bit odd. Granddad said that there were rumours that he was experimenting on genetically modified crops using animal and human genes.'

'That's just Oldport gossip,' Stephen Howley said.

'But what if Bukanov was working for him,' Jackie persisted. 'He was a geneticist. And Sean Gunne's father was a geneticist before he became a GP.'

Her father shook his head. 'Max Silvermann – or Hawk as he's better known – is a billionaire,' he said. 'Why would he need to imprison geneticists? And just because he's a recluse, doesn't mean he's an ogre. He's just a man who's trying to deal with the tragic death of his wife and young son. It can't be easy for him being crippled either.'

'Granddad told me about that,' Jackie said. 'His wife and son were killed in the car crash in Texas that left him crippled. Apparently Hawk was driving while drunk and blames himself for the accident.'

'So I've heard,' Stephen Howley said. 'But that doesn't make him a gaoler. Now then, I must get to work. Are you going into the office today?'

Jackie nodded. 'I'm meeting Sean Gunne later,' she said. 'Can I tell him what you've just told me?'

Her father hesitated. 'I suppose you can,' he said. 'The gardaí will be releasing all of it today. But ask him not to divulge any of it to anyone, just in case.'

'Thanks, Dad,' Jackie said. 'You're the best.'

On the way to the office Jackie thought about what she had learned. What her father said made sense. But deep down she had doubts. There simply were too many unanswered questions. What she needed was more information. Sergei Bukanov's death might have nothing to do with Sean's father's disappearance. Perhaps he had disappeared to save his own skin and the charges made against him were legitimate. But if not …? There was a mystery there and it was one that Jackie was determined to solve. But where to begin?

The first thing to do was to collect as much information as possible. So maybe she should start with Sergei Bukanov and Hawk Silvermann. There should be information on both of them on the Internet. Who knows? She might have even more interesting information for Sean Gunne when she met him later.

TEN

Costello sat at his desk, studying the report Corridan had compiled on Jackie Howley. What most interested Costello, and gave him most cause for concern, was the fact that

Stephen Howley was a security consultant. Did his daughter have the CD and if so, had she given it to her father? But if she had, why hadn't he handed it over to the police?

Was Howley contemplating blackmail? Costello knew so-called security consultants and investigators in New York who had blackmailed people with information that came their way. Many of those were small time operators like Stephen Howley. But few of them had ever had the opportunity that Howley now had if he possessed the CD.

Costello put down the report and picked up the newspapers. There was nothing new in any of them. Bukanov still hadn't been identified. What was new was a report on the local radio news bulletin that morning.

It stated that Bukanov had in his possession a small plastic bag which had been heat sealed. The bag had been torn open and, when found, was empty. The gardaí assumed that it had contained Bukanov's money and papers.

Costello knew this wasn't so. Bukanov had had neither papers nor money. What he did have was the CD, presumably in this sealed bag. So he hadn't lost it. He had torn open the bag himself and removed the CD. And then what ...?

Costello picked up the paper with the picture of Jackie Howley. If Bukanov had hidden the CD in the rucksack, then maybe she hadn't found it. Maybe it was still there.

When she checked the rucksack, she would have been checking to see if anything had been stolen. She could have had no reason to think that Bukanov might have put something in the bag. And with CDs already in the bag, it would have been easy to overlook an extra one slipped in among them.

Costello summoned Corridan. 'I want you to take Jordan,' he said, 'and go to Dublin. Find out all you can about this Howley girl and her father.'

'You think she has the CD?' Corridan asked.

Costello nodded. 'Yes. But I think she doesn't know that she has it. So it gives us a chance to get it back. Check out the house and the possibility of breaking in. Report back to me as soon as you've carried out a reconnaissance. I'll decide then what to do.'

+   +   +

That morning, Jackie Howley searched on the Internet for information on Sergei Bukanov. There were many pages and links with his name on them, all of the earlier ones relating to his work and to papers he had written on genetics.

In recent newspaper articles she found coverage of his attempt to get asylum in Britain and his subsequent refusal. After that there was nothing until reports of his death at Old-port. It was as if he had disappeared off the face of the earth until two days ago. She printed out the pieces she thought relevant and slipped the pages into an envelope. It was little enough to give Sean, but it was a beginning. Then she began her search for Max Silvermann.

Here the problem was too much information. She learned that his nickname, Hawk, had been given him by a journalist because he preyed on companies who were in financial difficulties. There were also reports of how he had come to be a billionaire, no two of them agreeing on the facts. It was the same story with the accident that had killed his son and his wife and crippled him.

There were conflicting reports too on his move to Fair Island. When he bought Fair Island from a famous pop star some years back, he already owned a number of factories in Ireland involved in the electronics and pharmaceutical industry. He visited the island regularly with his family, claiming that it was his sanctuary from the world of business.

After the death of his son, Abraham, he had come to live in the castle on Fair Island and had moved part of his extensive research and development arm to a new complex which he built beside the jetty. The dozen or so scientists and computer experts working there were said to be carrying out research into a computer that could be controlled by thought alone, a project Hawk had set up when he first became disabled. These scientists and experts lived at the complex during the week and returned to the mainland at weekends and for holidays. This was apparently intended to ensure secrecy, something Silvermann was obsessed with.

When she read this, Jackie couldn't suppress a tremor of excitement. Had Bukanov been working at the research complex on the island? Had he tried to steal some of the ideas? Was that why the men had been following him?

But it didn't make sense. If Bukanov had been employed there, then his colleagues would have contacted the gardaí when they learned of his death. But they hadn't done so. And the gardaí had already been informed that no one was missing from the island. So Bukanov couldn't have been working at the research complex.

Did that mean he was a spy, and that he had been on the island trying to steal secrets? From her father's work, Jackie knew that industrial espionage was a major problem for companies. Rivals were always interested in knowing what their competitors were doing. But if Bukanov had been spying on the island and had escaped, how had he reached the mainland? He didn't appear to have used a boat and surely it was too far to swim. Yet he *had* recently been in salt water.

She was getting nowhere and she had other matters to attend to. She printed out what she thought interesting and then concentrated on some typing for her father.

Sean came to see her later that morning and they went along to McDonald's for an early lunch. On the way she filled him in on all that she had learned so far.

'There's at least one link between Bukanov and my father,' he said. 'Both were geneticists.'

'I know,' Jackie said. 'But it could just be coincidence.'

Sean nodded, clearly doing his best to hide his disappointment as he took the printouts.

'It was a long shot,' he said resignedly. 'Bukanov has probably nothing to do with my father's disappearance. He was probably mumbling something in Russian.'

'Maybe,' Jackie said. 'But I think we should go there and make a few inquiries of our own.'

'To Russia!' Sean said in surprise.

Jackie laughed. 'Not Russia,' she said. 'Oldport.'

'Oh.' Sean laughed too and for a moment the sense of loss and disappointment left his eyes.

'Bukanov didn't appear out of thin air,' Jackie went on. 'So maybe we could find out where he did come from. Or what he was doing in Oldport.'

'Maybe he's still a terrorist,' Sean said. 'He could have been part of a team planning an attack.'

'In Ireland?' Jackie said in disbelief.

'He could have been planning it elsewhere and using Ireland as a base.'

'Maybe.' Jackie didn't sound convinced.

At McDonald's they ate in almost total silence. After a while Sean picked up the printouts and began to read. Suddenly he looked up. 'There *is* another link with my father,' he said excitedly.

'Yes?' Jackie sat up straight in her chair.

'Bukanov attended a scientific conference in Seattle some years ago. My father also attended a conference there. I remember because he said it reminded him of Ireland – that it rained all the time.'

'So you think they might have met each other there?' Jackie asked.

'It's possible, isn't it?' Sean said.

'I suppose,' Jackie agreed. 'But Bukanov would not have mentioned your father unless he'd met him recently. He'd hardly remember him from a conference held years ago.'

Sean looked despondent. Then he brightened. 'That's just it,' he said. 'He *must* have met him recently. You see, Liam only started calling him Doctor Dolittle after he became a GP. So Bukanov couldn't have known about the nickname at the time of the conference. Don't you see?'

'I see what you're getting at,' Jackie said. 'But why didn't Bukanov call your father Doctor Denis Gunne, or Doctor Gunne? Why Doctor Dolittle? I mean, would your father have even told him about his nickname?'

'He would,' Sean said. 'Whenever he spoke of Liam, he always referred to the nickname. So he would have told Bukanov about it. But I don't know why he might have used it. But then, he was dying, remember, and might not have known what he was saying …' He stopped, as if aware of the implications of his words.

'Look,' Jackie said. 'I think we should go to Oldport tomorrow and take a look around. We can stay overnight with Granddad Howley. What do you say?'

'I'll have to see,' Sean said. 'I couldn't leave my granddad alone overnight. A Mrs Carroll comes in a few times a day to check on him. She might be able to stay with him. Or his sister, Eileen, might be able to come over. She's not too well herself, but she does visit him regularly.'

'So you'll try and arrange something?' Jackie said. 'Then we can go to Oldport.'

'I suppose,' Sean said without enthusiasm.

'Right,' Jackie said. 'Could we meet later to discuss what we'll do there?'

'I could bring you round to my house this evening,' Sean suggested. 'Liam would love to meet you. I ... I told him about you and that you were helping me.'

'OK,' Jackie said. 'What time will you call?'

They agreed on a time and Sean headed off. Jackie watched until he disappeared. He had set off with his head high, but as he walked on his head drooped. She knew that he had already become despondent and had probably concluded that the trip to Oldport would be a waste of time.

Perhaps it would be, she thought. But then you could never be certain. Maybe they would find out something useful in Oldport and make some progress in solving the mystery.

ELEVEN

Jackie felt apprehensive at meeting Liam and his mother. As she and Sean turned into the street, she wished she hadn't come. But it was too late now to turn back. She sensed Sean's unease too, and that didn't help.

It was a street of semi-detached houses secluded by hedges,

the green foliage so dark as to be almost black. Sean's house was red bricked and obviously old. The lawn was neatly mown, the borders a riot of colour – vibrant blues and greens and red and purples. Geraniums grew profusely in pots on either side of the door and in wooden window boxes.

The entrance hall was dominated by a grandfather clock without hands. On a hall table stood a colourful flower arrangement that gave the impression that the garden had encroached within. Jackie followed Sean down the hall, past a sitting room and into a large airy kitchen. A tall thin woman stood at the sink. She turned towards them, a partly peeled potato in her hand. She wore a dark trouser suit and her dark hair was cropped short.

'You must be Jackie,' she said warmly. 'Sean's told us all about you.'

Jackie blushed. 'Hel ... hello, Mrs Gunne,' she mumbled.

'Call me Beatrice.' Sean's mother smiled in a friendly way. 'If you're looking for Liam, you'll find him in his den. You will stay to dinner, won't you?'

'I... I don't ...' Jackie tried.

'She will, Mom,' Sean said. 'Now come on, Jackie. Liam's mad to meet you.'

He led her through an arch into the small dining room and through open French doors into a sunroom. With its profusion of flowers and greenery, it was like an indoor extension of the garden. At the far end, before the open door leading into the garden, she saw the back of a wheelchair.

As she drew near she saw a thatch of dark hair. But its owner showed no sign of being aware of their presence. He wore headphones, wires trailing down to a portable CD player attached to the side of the chair.

A black cat sat in his lap and looked lazily up at their

approach. It must have alerted Liam to their presence for he twisted his head about and rolled his eyes upwards to look at them. He obviously couldn't raise his head and his efforts to see them gave him a mischievous look.

Immediately his face lit up. With his right hand he removed the headphones, which he dropped on top of the cat. But the dark creature took no notice. 'Ah ha,' he said. 'So this is your latest girlfriend.'

'Liam!' Sean exclaimed. 'Didn't I warn you?' His words carried a reprimand, but his voice was gentle and affectionate. 'You mustn't embarrass Jackie.'

'Mustn't embarrass you, you mean,' Liam laughed. He reached for the joystick fitted to the arm of the chair and turned about to face them. He was looking up at Jackie, his piercing blue eyes taking in everything about her.

In other circumstances she would have felt uncomfortable or embarrassed. But there was an innocence in those blue eyes, an openness she had only ever encountered in very young children, never before in a boy of ten.

Sean moved forward to hug his brother. 'Another word out of you,' he threatened, 'and I'll put you and Killer out in the garden. So behave.' He straightened up and indicated Jackie. 'I suppose I'd better introduce you two,' he added. 'Liam, meet Jackie Howley.'

Liam raised his hand and Jackie proffered her own. His grip was firm. 'We are delighted to meet you, Jackie Howley,' he said in a very formal voice. 'Killer and I, both of us, are absolutely delighted.'

At this the cat stared up at her and meowed. For a moment there was silence. Then the three burst into spontaneous laughter. 'I warned you he was mad,' Sean said to Jackie between bursts of mirth. 'But you wouldn't believe me.'

'I rather think she reserved her judgement until we became acquainted,' Liam said. 'Quite the correct thing to do.'

'Don't mind that silly accent and his funny way of speaking,' Sean said. 'He listens to PG Wodehouse stories all the time. He thinks he's Jeeves.'

'Do you mind!' Liam said in mock indignation. 'Not Jeeves, old boy. He's a mere servant. I rather like to think of myself as Bertie Wooster. Now, kindly leave us.'

'You behave,' Sean said. 'Or else …' He turned to Jackie, his face still creased with laughter lines. 'I'll go and help Mum. If he keeps up that posh accent,' he went on, 'hit him over the head. It's the only thing that seems to work.'

She knew Sean was trying to put her at her ease. But it wasn't working. As Sean walked away, she was tempted to follow.

'He misses our father,' Liam said, breaking into her thoughts. 'We both do.'

She turned back towards him, registering the sadness in his eyes. 'It must be terrible for you all,' she said. 'Not knowing …'

'That and the lies,' he said. 'They're almost as bad. Dad was … is a good man. He would never sell drugs. But just to see the headlines …'

He reached down to stroke the cat, which raised its head to nuzzle against him. Jackie stood silent, watching him. After a moment he looked up. 'Oh, I am sorry,' he said. 'Bertie Wooster would never dream of leaving a lady standing. He would have Jeeves provide a chair for her. Alas it's Jeeves' day off so you'll have to provide your own. You don't mind?'

'No,' Jackie laughed. 'I have to provide my own at home since our butler left.'

'I knew you were a good sport,' Liam laughed, as Jackie pulled over a wicker chair and sat down. 'Sean isn't so glum since he met you. I'm glad of that. He is my favourite brother, but then he has no competition.' His eyes twinkled as he spoke. 'So, tell me all about yourself.'

Jackie recounted a bare outline of her life. Liam listened, not interrupting once, and she could tell that he missed nothing. He might play the fool, but there was an acute intelligence at work behind the facade.

'So you're going to help Sean find our father,' he said when she'd finished.

'I'm going to try,' she said. 'But we've so little to go on. There's really only ...' She stopped, not wanting to upset him.

'It's OK,' he said. 'I understand. But it's just that we cling to any bit of hope. And I should be apologising to you. It's too nice an evening to be talking of gloomy matters. Come outside and I'll show you the garden.'

She followed the chair, which he manoeuvred with consummate skill through the open door and onto a paved patio. Here were rows of wooden troughs, raised on trestles, each one a riot of colour. He pointed out and named the flowers: begonias in pinks and reds and oranges, fleshy dahlias in yellows and the lightest shades of pink, geraniums in vivid reds and blues and whites. She accompanied him up and down the rows as he deadheaded a flower here and there or picked off a discoloured leaf.

A ramp led down into the garden where a network of paved footpaths ran off at right angles from a central path. On either side of the paths, in raised brick-built beds, flowers blazed in the sunshine. The garden seemed alive with the hum of bees and she caught the heady scent of perfume on the warm air.

She followed Liam along the central path towards the end of the garden. Here a greenhouse and garden shed stood behind a low wooden fence. They entered through a wooden gate, designed in two halves to swing open in either direction.

Jackie found herself in a fruit and vegetable garden with dwarf fruit trees growing either side of the central path. Here again, further paths branched off the main artery at right angles. These too were lined with raised beds in which vegetables grew. She recognised onions and cabbages and lettuces and the delicate greenery of young carrots.

Liam burrowed with his fingers in one of the beds. 'It's been warm today,' he said. 'They'll need watering later.'

'This is all your doing?' Jackie said in astonishment. 'It's fantastic.'

'I grew watercress when I was three,' Liam said, turning the chair to face her. 'It grows quickly and I thought it was the most fantastic thing I ever saw in my life. After that I was hooked. I spend all my spare time out here. I grow all the fruit and vegetables we need for the house.'

There was no mistaking the pride in his voice. As Jackie stared at him in admiration, he blushed and looked away. 'If you wouldn't mind nipping into the shed you'll find some cardboard boxes,' he said. 'You might get one for me.'

She located a box from a number that were stacked neatly in the shed. 'You like lettuce?' he asked when she returned and she nodded. 'You hold the box,' he went on, 'and follow me.'

He selected a head of lettuce and scallions and a bunch of baby carrots and placed them in the box. A larger head of dark green cabbage took up most of the remaining space. 'Next time you call,' he said, 'I'll give you more. OK?'

'OK,' she said. 'I'm very grateful.'

'They're all organically grown,' he said, the pride still in his voice. 'When my Dad built the beds, he got the soil from an organic farm. It had to be barrowed in from the street. He spent a whole summer doing it ...'

His voice trailed off and he looked down and stroked the cat.

It purred contentedly in response. Jackie stayed silent. 'Why would someone like that get involved in drugs?' Liam went on. 'It's why I wanted you to see the garden. I'm not showing off my work. I wanted you to see what sort of man my father is.'

Jackie was almost moved to tears by his love for his father. In many ways he seemed older than Sean.

'Good,' he said. 'Now we'll go back inside. Dinner should be ready. And I'm sure Sean will want your company to himself.'

'I ...' was all she could manage, blushing furiously.

'Sorry,' Liam said. 'Bertie Wooster promises to behave himself from now on. So shall we proceed indoors, my dear, and partake of dinner.'

The accent was perfect, exactly like that of an English toff in an old black and white film. Jackie burst out laughing. 'Jolly good,' Liam said. 'That's the spirit.'

She followed him back into the house. Sean was laying the table while Mrs Gunne busied herself at the cooker in the kitchen. 'I'll do that, Sean,' Liam offered. 'You'll want to show Jackie your books and music. I only hope you tidied your room, old chap, otherwise you'll be letting the Woosters down.'

Sean picked up a tea towel and threw it at his brother. 'Give me those,' he said to Jackie, taking the box of vegetables. 'I'll put them away until you're ready to leave.'

She followed him into the hall. He placed the box at the foot of the stairs and began to climb, beckoning Jackie to follow. Despite what Liam had said, Sean's room was neat and tidy.

'You like Limp Bizkit?' he asked. 'I've got their latest album.' She nodded and he took a CD from a revolving rack and slotted it into a player. As the music began, the volume low, he turned to her. 'So what do you think of Liam?' he asked.

'He's fantastic,' she said. 'And his garden's brilliant.'

'The garden's his life,' Sean said. 'It's what he would like to do – you know, later ...' He trailed off and stared from the window overlooking the street.

'There's no reason why he couldn't,' she said. 'Is there?'

'His condition is deteriorating,' Sean said quietly. 'That's what happens. This will be his last year in the garden. By next summer the doctors say he'll have lost the power of his hands.'

'Oh.' She remembered the happiness in Liam's face when he talked about his garden. She shivered despite the warmth. 'But he could still enjoy the garden,' she said. 'Someone could do the actual physical work. It's his knowledge that counts. You could do it for him. I ... I could come and help.'

Sean turned towards her. 'Of course I'll help him,' he said. 'I'd do anything for him. But it's not that.' He stared at her. In the background, the music played

'What is it?' she said, sensing his pain.

'It's the disease,' he said. 'There's no cure for the rare condition Sean has – nothing can halt its progress.'

'So what you're saying is that a time will come when he will be virtually helpless?'

'Two years, the doctors say,' Sean said, still speaking quietly. 'Three at the most. For some reason he's deteriorating more quickly than is usual.'

'And there's nothing they can do?'

He shook his head and she wanted to reach out her hand to comfort him. 'That's terrible,' she said. 'For all of you. But Liam is the only one who really matters. You'll all just have to be brave for him.'

His eyes narrowed and she realised she was missing something. 'What is it?' she asked again, and then the reality of what he was implying hit her. 'You don't ...' she said. 'You can't mean ... '

'I'm sorry,' he said. 'I didn't mean to upset you. But you see, the disease attacks all the muscles, so his heart is affected too. The best medical estimate is that Liam has six years at the very most. But it's more likely to be less. What's almost certain is that he will be dead by his sixteenth birthday.'

TWELVE

On Fair Island, Costello opened the door of the black hole, allowing the harsh glare of the single light bulb hanging outside to flood the cell. Denis Gunne sat on his haunches, his hand raised to his face to shield his eyes from the light. Already there was a stench from the cell and Costello clamped his fingers to his nose.

He prodded Gunne's thigh with the toe of his shoe. 'You ready to work yet?' he asked.

Gunne didn't reply and Costello prodded him a second time. Then he drew back his foot and kicked Gunne in the ribs, drawing a gasp of pain. 'Answer me,' Costello said. 'Are you ready to work?'

'No,' Gunne said, quietly but firmly. 'When you bring a message from my sons – and one I know to be genuine – then I'll consider working.'

Costello swore under his breath and kicked Gunne twice more in the ribs. Then he stepped back and slammed the door shut and locked it.

Back in his room, he sat at his desk, mulling over the situation. Gunne, he knew, was much stronger than Bukanov, if not physically then mentally. He might last a whole month or more in the black hole without breaking. And even when he broke – and Costello didn't doubt that he could be broken – he might not be capable of work. Then it would all have been for nothing.

Costello wanted results and he wanted them soon. Hawk's promise of an even larger bonus if progress could be made before he moved his operation seemed to dangle continuously before Costello's eyes. Gunne was the only obstacle in the way.

'We need his expertise,' Brandt had explained earlier when Costello had raised the matter. 'A geneticist is essential to the project's success.'

For a while Costello had considered abducting another geneticist. But as Hawk had pointed out, that would be foolish. It was likely to draw attention to the death of the other geneticist in Oldport. Then it would be but a matter of time before someone began to ask questions and to focus attention on Fair Island, especially as rumours persisted that genetic research was already being carried out at the research complex.

Costello's thoughts were interrupted by the telephone. It was Corridan reporting from Dublin. 'The girl left the house fifteen minutes ago,' he said. 'It's now vacant as far as I tell. Do you want me to see if I can locate the CD?'

Costello hesitated. This might be their best chance. But it would take time to do a thorough search for the CD if it had been hidden. And the girl or her father might return at any time. Could Corridan act safely in broad daylight? He put the question to him.

'There's a side entrance,' Corridan explained. 'And the rear garden is pretty secluded. I think it could be done.'

'OK,' Costello decided. 'Do it.'

'Right,' Corridan said. 'I'm just going to drive around one more time and make sure that ...' He trailed off. 'Damn!' he went on. 'Howley has just returned. His car's pulled into the driveway.'

'You sure it's him?' Costello asked.

'Yeah, it's him,' Corridan said. 'What now, boss?'

'Keep a watch on the house,' Costello said, his voice filled with his frustration. 'If you get a chance tonight, take it. If not, wait until tomorrow.'

'Right,' Corridan said, and he cut the connection.

Costello sat quietly for a few moments. The most pressing problem right now was to locate the CD. Once that was accomplished, he could consider the matter of getting Gunne's co-operation.

As he rose to his feet, he had come to one decision. When Hawk moved his operation to another country, one person would not be travelling with him, willingly or unwillingly. When the time came Costello would have his revenge. Gunne would become food for the fishes.

Buoyed a little by the prospect, Costello went along to the laboratories. Since Hawk had promised the extra bonus, Costello had taken a more personal interest in the work being done by the scientists.

'Stewart is continuing to do good work,' Brandt told him. 'But we really need Doctor Gunne's expertise to ensure that we continue that progress.' He reached out to adjust a dial on one of his machines.

Costello nodded. 'I'm working on that,' he said. 'I think you will have his co-operation soon.'

'Very good,' Brandt said. 'I hope so.'

Costello left the laboratory and returned to his quarters.

Perhaps things weren't as black as he had first thought. If Corridan recovered the CD and Gunne agreed to co-operate, then all would be well again.

But if not, there was little that Costello could do about the missing CD except hope that it never turned up. Getting Gunne to work with them was a different matter. He would give him another while in the black hole and if he hadn't broken by then, Costello would have to consider another strategy.

Already an idea was forming at the back of his mind. If it was carried out properly, then there should be no danger involved. He needed to break Gunne if that bonus promised by Hawk was to become a reality. And break him he would, one way or the other.

+   +   +

Sean accompanied Jackie to the bus stop. They were both silent on the walk. It was as if what Jackie had learned had formed a barrier between them. At the bus stop, Sean suggested accompanying her home, but Jackie declined his offer. She wanted to be alone with her thoughts, and to try and come to terms with the awful reality that Liam would die.

Sean seemed to sense her mood and accepted her decision without demur. They said goodbye, agreeing to meet at the railway station early the next morning. But even now Jackie's confidence of finding out anything at Oldport was waning.

Sean walked away and at the end of the street, turned to wave. She waved once and then he turned the corner and was lost from sight.

On the bus, Jackie rested the box of vegetables on her knees. It was difficult to accept the fact that the boy who had shown her the garden – who had grown the vegetables she carried – would be dead by the time she completed her secondary education.

She had not enjoyed her dinner, though it was fancier and different from what she was used to at home. What she had just learned about Liam had spoiled it for her.

He had supplied the only relief. He talked non-stop about vegetables and books and farmyard manure and music, as if they all belonged together quite naturally. He was a fount of knowledge on the latest music scene and wasn't afraid to voice his opinions, which were blunt and to the point.

Mrs Gunne and Sean had both eaten quietly. Denis Gunne was never mentioned. Nor was any reference made to what Jackie had witnessed on Sunday. Mrs Gunne served dessert – fresh strawberries and cream. While the others ate, she busied herself loading the dishwasher and tidying the kitchen.

Jackie found this disconcerting. Her father always insisted she remain at the table until he, or anyone else who might be there, had finished their meal. 'Good company is more impor tant that a tidy kitchen,' he would say. 'It's bad manners to leave the table before everyone has eaten.'

But it wasn't bad manners that had driven Mrs Gunne from the table, Jackie realised, but unhappiness. It was a sad house, yet she had a sense that once it had been joyful and filled with laughter. Could it be so again, even if only for the few years Liam had to live?

As the bus dropped her off, Jackie had found a new sense of purpose again. She would do everything in her power to find Doctor Gunne and hopefully bring back some of that happi ness and joy to the family. And tomorrow, by going to Oldport, she would take the first step to achieving just that.

She turned into her street and made her way along to her house. As she opened the front door, she had a sense of being watched, and turned to look out on the darkening street. But as she did so, her father called out to her: 'Is that you, Jackie?'

'Yes, Dad,' she said. 'It's me.' She closed the door and hurried into the kitchen. Her father sat at the table, some papers before him. Jackie placed the box on the table and then threw her arms about him.

'What's all this?' he laughed.

She didn't answer, but pressed her head against his shoulder as the first tears welled up in her eyes. His arms clasped her to him and she clung to his warmth and security. She felt like the little girl she had been when her mother died and who had known then that her father was the only one who could make the world all right.

THIRTEEN

The next morning at the railway station, Jackie noted that Sean was very down. As the train moved off and he sat staring out at the drab Dublin suburbs, she tried to cheer him up. But it had no effect. 'There's nothing I can do for my father,' Sean said despairingly. 'Or for Liam. I realised that last night.'

'But aren't you doing something now?' Jackie insisted.

'It'll be a waste of time,' Sean said. 'There's probably no link between my father and Bukanov. Even you didn't think there was one.'

'I know,' Jackie said. 'But I've changed my mind. I think now that they must have met. Otherwise, as you've already pointed out, how did Bukanov know your father's nickname? I think Bukanov was a prisoner somewhere and he escaped. Those men at the railway station were trying to re-capture him.'

'But he chose to risk his life rather than give himself up,' Sean said, a tremor in his voice. 'That's how desperate he was. And if he was that desperate and those men are also holding my father prisoner ...' He let the words trail off. Their implication that his father could be in grave danger was obvious.

They grew silent. Both stared out of the window as they left the suburbs behind and sped through the flat green fields of the midlands. 'Oldport holds the key,' Jackie said, when she could bear the silence no longer. 'That's where Bukanov surfaced. I'm certain your father's there too – that's where they met.'

'But why would anyone kidnap two scientists and hold them prisoner?' Sean said.

'I don't know,' Jackie shrugged. 'But both were expert geneticists. Someone must have wanted their knowledge for some reason.'

'But why abduct them? Why not just employ two geneticists?'

'Because what they're doing is illegal. Or they can't afford to pay.'

'Or they're mad.'

'Could be,' Jackie agreed.

'I wonder if there are others?' Sean said, almost to himself.

'Others?' Jackie looked puzzled. 'What do you mean?'

'Other missing scientists,' Sean said. 'I wonder if any other scientist have gone missing?'

'That's a good point,' Jackie said. 'Is there anyway we could find out?' She sat upright, frowning in concentration, and tapped her fingers on the table.

'I don't know,' Sean said.

'Let's think it through,' Jackie said. 'Now, if we assume that your father first met Bukanov at that Seattle conference, then they both must have met most, if not all of the other scientists who were there. Now suppose whoever abducted your father and Bukanov also met those other scientists. He might have abducted some of them too. For all we know, he might have taken all of them. Maybe they're all working for a terrorist organisation, building some secret biological weapon.'

'Maybe,' Sean said doubtfully.

'Well, we can check on that Internet site for the names of all those who attended that conference,' Jackie said. 'Then we can check individually to see if any of them is missing.'

'I hadn't thought of that,' Sean said. For the first time he sounded optimistic. Jackie sat back, relieved and not a little excited. The hunt was on.

The library in Oldport had three computers connected to the Internet. Two were being used and Jackie was informed that the third one was booked. She couldn't hide her disappointment and the librarian smiled sympathetically. 'We'll give the booking five minutes,' the woman said. 'If they're not here by then, you can use it.'

Five minutes later, Jackie got access to the computer. While Sean sat beside her, she found the site featuring the Seattle conference. Five other scientists were named and, with subsequent searches, she found references to all of them. But there was no mention of their being missing.

Jackie now followed a trail through sites and pages and links, too numerous to be checked out in the allotted time. She was about to give up and was scrolling down a new list of searches, when Sean grabbed her hand. 'Go back,' he said, his voice quivering with excitement.

Jackie scrolled back up the page. 'There!' Sean exclaimed, tapping the screen with his finger. There were four words in bold letters: 'MYSTERY OF MISSING SCIENTIST'. It was a report from a newspaper, *The Scot's Inquirer*. Her hand trembling, Jackie moved the cursor over the cached pages and clicked.

The report stated that James Stewart, a leading expert on molecular biology and cell division, had disappeared. Mr Stewart, who worked at The Glasgow Institute, had been offered a position with a company, Mirror Image, in San Antonio, Texas, four months ago. He had gone there for an interview and later phoned his wife, from whom he was being divorced, to say that he was accepting the position. He was never heard from again. Subsequent police inquiries in San Antonio proved that no such company ever existed.

During their investigations, the police discovered that Mr Stewart owed huge gambling debts to a notorious Glasgow crime boss who had threatened his life. There was no evidence that Mr Stewart's disappearance was linked to this, but the police stated that they were keeping an open mind on the matter.

Jackie and Sean stared at each other. 'There has to be a link,' Jackie said, unable to hide her excitement. 'We'll find it and then ...' She stopped and stared at Sean who, though obviously sharing her excitement, suddenly seemed upset. 'What is it?' she asked

'It's to do with a terrible row between my mother and father,' Sean said quietly. 'Dad was offered a research job in the US some months ago, which he turned down. Shortly after that, the drug addicts started coming to the surgery. My mother begged him to reconsider the offer. She was willing for us all to get back together if we could go to the US and make a new start. But Dad still refused.'

'But what's that got to do with this man, Stewart?' Jackie asked.

'I can't remember the name of the company,' Sean said. 'But I do remember where it was based: San Antonio, Texas.'

Jackie was struck dumb. She took some moments to recover her voice. 'But that's it,' she said. 'That's the link. Stewart and your father are research scientists. Both were offered jobs with a company in San Antonio, and both have disappeared.'

'But my father never went to San Antonio,' Sean said, his initial euphoria evaporating. 'So how can his disappearance be linked to Stewart's? And if Stewart disappeared in Texas, what can that have to do with Oldport?'

'I don't know,' Jackie said, shaking her head in frustration. 'But don't forget Hawk Silvermann is a Texan. And there is one other link between your father, Bukanov and Stewart.'

'What link? I can't see any.'

'They were all in trouble of one kind or another,' she said quietly, avoiding Sean's eyes.

'But my father is innocent,' Sean said angrily. 'I told you that.'

'I'm not doubting it,' Jackie said quietly. 'I'm just saying that he was in trouble, just like Bukanov and Stewart. Don't you see? Bukanov was denied asylum and was being deported to Russia, where he would be tried as a terrorist and possibly executed. A criminal was threatening Stewart's life because he owed him money. Your father was accused of supplying drugs. If charges were brought against him and he was found guilty, he would go to prison. Don't you see,' she went on vehemently, 'the three of them had good reason to disappear.'

Sean remained silent and Jackie took a deep breath. 'It doesn't mean your father is guilty,' she continued. 'I believe you when you say he's innocent. But if he is innocent, then someone framed him.'

Sean was nodding agreement now. 'I'm sorry,' he said. 'I do understand what you're saying. And you could be right. It's just that when I hear any suggestion that my father might have done something wrong …'

He trailed off and Jackie stayed silent. Just then the librarian approached and told them their time was up. They thanked her and went back out into the sunshine. 'Come on,' Jackie said. 'Let's go to Granddad's. I'm starved.'

Peter Howley lived alone in a large detached house on the outskirts of Oldport. A tall grey-haired man, he welcomed both of them warmly. 'I'd say you'd be hungry,' he said, when Jackie had made the introductions. 'So let's have some lunch.'

They retreated to the kitchen where Jackie helped the old man prepare a salad. 'So what brings you two to Oldport?' he asked. 'I thought we wouldn't see you again for ages, Jackie.'

'Oh, just visiting,' Jackie said, having already agreed with Sean that they wouldn't divulge the reason for their visit to anyone.

'Showing the boyfriend around, is it?'

'Granddad!' Jackie said, blushing.

'Sorry,' the old man chuckled. 'Me and my big mouth. Now let's eat.'

As they sat at the pine table, Mr Howley switched on a portable television. 'See what's on the news,' he said.

The third news item dealt with Sunday's incident and the three gave it their full attention. But there was little new until the final item, which drew gasps from Sean and Jackie. Peter Howley stared at them in amazement.

'In 1977,' the reporter said, 'Sergei Bukanov was tipped to be the next Olympic breaststroke champion. But that was before a serious injury interrupted his career. This new information now adds further credence to speculation that he may have swum ashore from a trawler or other boat on Sunday morning in a last desperate attempt to avoid deportation to Russia.'

FOURTEEN

After lunch Jackie showed Sean his bedroom. It was in the attic, with sea views, and as he stared from the window at Fair Island, he wondered if his father was a prisoner in the castle. And if so, what purpose could an American billionaire have for abducting research scientists?

There was a knock on the door. Jackie poked her head in. 'Come on,' she said. 'I'll ask Granddad if we can go fishing. He always takes me out when I'm here. And we can get a look at the island from the boat.'

They went back downstairs and Jackie made her request. Peter Howley, a keen fisherman himself, was only too glad to oblige. Jackie made some sandwiches and after emptying her clothes out of her rucksack, put them in there along with a big bottle of mineral water. Then they set off for Oldport jetty.

Once they'd donned their life jackets, Peter Howley set a course for the open sea. Jackie, whom her grandfather had taught to handle a boat as soon as she could walk, took over the helm, while Peter and Sean prepared their fishing tackle.

Jackie headed for Fair Island and, two kilometres off shore, cut the engine. While Sean and Peter Howley began to fish, Jackie took her grandfather's binoculars and, hooding the lens so that they didn't reflect the sunlight, trained them on the island.

It was about three kilometres long and a kilometre wide. Part of the south shore was sheer cliff, about thirty metres high. On the very edge stood the castle, its tower a dark finger stub pointing to the sky.

'Fancy owning a whole island,' Jackie said, joining the two fishermen. 'Silvermann must be fabulously rich.'

'He's a billionaire,' Peter Howley said.

'I've heard he's mad,' Jackie said, 'and that he's got slaves on the island.'

'That's just one of the sillier rumours,' her grandfather laughed. 'No one really believes it.'

'So what are these other rumours?' Jackie asked.

'Oh, anything and everything, if the truth be told. Some claim that Mr Silvermann has built a bunker on the island capable of withstanding a nuclear attack. Others say that he's the leader of a secret sect and has built an underground church as big as a cathedral. There's even a rumour that he's trying to develop a computer chip to implant in his brain to cure his paralysis. Mind you, they're the rumours you could half believe. But the one about the bunker is possibly true. I read somewhere that most very rich men have built one beneath their property.'

Sean was only half listening. His thoughts were on that rumour about Hawk trying to develop a computer chip to cure his paralysis. Could it be true? If it were true, then that would explain why medical research scientists were required for the project. But why would he need to kidnap scientists to do it? That sort of research could be carried out quite openly. Why keep it secret?

Were there some horrific, illegal experiments involved? Sean knew from his father's research that animals were used in medical experiments. It was just one of the many reasons why his father had got out of research. Could Hawk be carrying out such experiments, not on animals – that after all was legal – but on humans? Sean shivered at the thought.

'Can we circle the island?' Jackie asked. 'I'm sure Sean would like to see it.'

'Go on, then,' Peter Howley said. 'There's good fishing on the western side. We'll try our luck there.'

'Here's some binoculars,' Jackie said to Sean as she opened the throttle.

They passed the southern tip and swung north, heading towards the wider part of the island. The sea was choppy here and the boat rode the swell like a roller-coaster. Sean watched the island through the binoculars as they passed, seeing the tower from the other side and also the extensive range of other buildings built beside it.

A high chain link fence, topped with razor wire, enclosed the complex on three sides. The fourth side, formed by the southern wall of the tower, overlooked the cliff. Heavy steel gates set into the northern side of the chain link fence were the only means of access to the complex. Sean saw movement behind the fence and, training the glasses there, saw two Rottweilers prowling the perimeter. Even from this distance they made him uneasy.

Jackie cut the engine. They were still about two kilometres off shore, opposite a jetty where a large cruiser, 'Spirit of Abraham', was tied up. Near the jetty was the newly built research and development division, a complex of white steel-clad buildings, fenced off in the same way as the castle complex. Clearly someone was determined that no one should get inside. Or maybe that no one inside should escape?

'Come on then,' Peter Howley said. 'Let's catch some fish.'

Sean's heart wasn't in it. He desperately wanted to get onto the island and look for his father. But he couldn't do that in broad daylight; it would have to be at night. And even if he did get onto the island, what then? He could never gain access to the castle, not with that fence and the patrolling dogs. Despair settled on his shoulders and even when he caught his first three mackerel, he felt no elation.

'Don't be so glum,' Jackie said, 'and I'll treat you to an ice-cream sundae in 'Romano's' when we get back to Oldport. They have the best sundaes in Ireland.'

+   +   +

The lookout Costello had posted as a precaution kept his binoculars trained on the boat and its occupants. He could see they were watching the island through binoculars, but he didn't consider an old man and two young people much of a threat. However, Costello's orders were to report anyone approaching the island or showing an interest in it. Sighing, the lookout reached for the walkie-talkie clipped to his belt.

On being informed of what was happening, Costello hurried to the lookout post and took the binoculars. He trained them on the boat for some minutes, before handing them back, his face a mask of anger and disbelief. 'Keep them under surveillance,' he ordered the lookout. 'Inform me immediately of any change in their behaviour.' His voice carried authority, but as he returned to the control centre, his mind was agitated.

He had recognised both teenagers: the Howley girl from the recent photographs in the papers, and Gunne's son from a photograph his father had in his wallet when they'd taken him. But the old man was unknown to him. He was probably the girl's grandfather whom he'd read about in the newspapers. As he sat in the control centre, Costello wondered what they were doing here, spying on the island. What had they found out? And how did Gunne's son know the girl who'd been at Oldport station on Sunday morning?

Had the girl found Bukanov's CD in her rucksack? But if she had, surely she would have handed it over to the police? Or maybe she gave it to her father, the security consultant? He would recognise its moneymaking value. But then what was Gunne's son doing here? He would hardly go along with blackmail. He would want to find his father and release him.

Costello felt certain that Bukanov must have put the CD in the rucksack. But it wasn't in her house. Corridan and Jordan had spent a fruitless morning searching for it. So where was it?

Costello picked up the phone and summoned Granger, one of his security staff. He ordered the man to take Cooney, another member of the security team, with him to the mainland. When the occupants of the boat returned to shore they were to follow the teenagers, find out where they were staying and report back.

+   +   +

Granger and Cooney watched the fishing boat dock. The old man stayed aboard while the two young people headed for the town centre. Both men followed their quarry to a fast food outlet called 'Romano's'.

The two men approached the premises and watched the pair through the window. The place was busy and the girl threw her rucksack onto one of the few vacant tables before joining her companion in the queue.

Granger took out his mobile phone and reported to Costello. 'Stay with them,' Costello said. 'I want to know where they're staying or if they take the train to Dublin.'

'They've no luggage,' Granger said. 'Just a rucksack belonging to the girl.'

'What? Did you say a rucksack? A red one?'

'Yeah,' Granger said.

'I want that rucksack,' Costello said. 'Don't let it or the girl out of your sight. Report to me every ten minutes. Understood?'

'Sure,' Granger said again. He cut the connection and stared through the window. The teenagers were still four or five from the counter. He glanced at the rucksack on the table. It was there to be picked up, but he couldn't do it without being noticed. Now, if he could create a diversion ...

An idea was forming in Granger's mind. He turned to Cooney to explain what he proposed. Cooney nodded and the two men entered the restaurant. Granger headed for the door marked Toilets. Cooney casually walked over towards the table on which the rucksack lay.

Granger grunted in satisfaction when he entered the toilets and saw the smoke detector fitted to the ceiling. Tearing off a strip of paper towel, he locked himself in one of the cubicles. He crunched up the paper, then lit it with his lighter. It burned easily, and when a trickle of smoke began to curl upwards, he stood on the toilet and thrust the burning paper up near the smoke detector.

An alarm went off almost immediately, its strident note piercing the air. Granger dropped the burning paper, unlocked the cubicle door and hurried from the toilets as sprinklers fitted in the ceiling began to douse everyone and everything.

As customers screamed in panic and frightened staff tried to evacuate the premises in an orderly fashion, Granger walked quickly through the restaurant and out onto the street. Cooney was already outside, the red rucksack tucked beneath his arm. They did not speak as they headed for the pier and the boat back to Fair Island.

+   +   +

Thirty minutes after the alarm went off, Jackie was allowed inside to retrieve her belongings. The manager was explaining to angry, soaked customers how the alarm had been set off and threatening dire consequences for the vandal responsible.

Having been at the end of the queue, and already on their feet, Jackie and Sean had been able to vacate the premises quickly. So they were no wetter than if they had been caught in a light rain shower.

When Jackie got to the table, there was no sign of her rucksack. She immediately informed a member of staff who, after a quick search, summoned a harassed looking supervisor.

'Someone must have picked it up by mistake in the confusion,' he said. 'When they realise their mistake they'll bring it back. Leave your telephone number with me and I'll ring you as soon as it's returned.'

She had to be satisfied with this and, leaving the restaurant, joined Sean outside. Quickly she explained to him what had happened. 'Come on,' she said. 'Let's go and get a sundae somewhere else.'

They were eating their sundaes when Jackie's mobile rang. She unclipped it from her belt and her face registered shock as she listened. When she cut the connection, her face was pale. 'That was my father,' she said to Sean. 'There was a burglary at our house earlier today.'

'A burglary?' he said. 'Oh my God! What did they steal?'

'That's just it,' Jackie said. 'Nothing seems to be missing. But my room and the sitting room and Dad's study were ransacked. All our CDs and CD ROMs and Dad's writeable CDs were thrown about. He's investigating a security leak at a computer software company just now – someone's been pirating their products – and he thinks the pirates were responsible, that they were looking for any computer disks containing evidence.'

She looked thoughtful. 'Doesn't it strike you as being too much of a coincidence, though? There's a burglary at my house earlier today and hours later my rucksack goes missing.'

'I hadn't thought of it like that,' Sean said. 'But you could be right. Maybe the piracy people think that your dad might have given a disk to you for safekeeping,' he suggested, without much conviction.

'No.' Jackie shook her head. 'He would never involve me. Anyone would know that. This has to do with Bukanov and your father. I don't think the fire was started by a vandal. I think someone deliberately set the fire so they could steal my rucksack.'

'But why?' Sean was clearly puzzled.

'Because they thought there was something in it,' Jackie said quietly

'But I don't understand,' he said. 'What do you mean: something in it? What could be in it that they would want?'

'Whatever Bukanov put in it on Sunday morning.'

Sean stared at her in amazement.

'I've been thinking about it,' Jackie said. 'We've all assumed that Bukanov was trying to steal from my rucksack – that he was looking for money. But why didn't he just grab it and run? It's what any thief would have done. So maybe he wasn't trying to *take* something; he was trying to *give* me something. He was trying to hide something in the rucksack – something he didn't want those men to find.'

'But what could he have been hiding?' Sean asked. 'And how come you haven't found it?'

'I don't know,' Jackie said. 'I took out my clothes when I got back home last Sunday and I didn't notice anything odd among them. Nor among my CDs. But the rucksack has half a dozen or more zipped pockets at the front and the sides. Bukanov could have put something in there. Don't forget that he had a small, heat-sealed bag with him. It must have contained something. Whatever it was, it was never found. If he slipped something small into a pocket in my rucksack I would never have noticed it there unless I was actually looking for it.'

'I realise that,' Sean said. 'But he could simply have lost whatever it was he had in the bag.'

'Maybe,' Jackie agreed. 'But the bag was torn open. That didn't happen by accident. Bukanov must have torn it open to take out whatever was in it. And I think he then hid that in my rucksack. And whoever has just taken the rucksack came to the same conclusion. It must implicate them and they had to get it back.'

'I don't know ...' Sean was not fully convinced. 'Maybe we should go to the guards,' he suggested, 'and report the theft.'

'Let's wait and see if the rucksack might have been taken by mistake,' Jackie said. 'If it was, then we can check if it does contain anything. If it isn't returned, then we'll know that someone stole it. OK?'

Sean nodded, his face showing concern. 'If you're right,' he said, 'do you realise what it means? If it's the same people who broke into your house, and who've now stolen your rucksack, then they must have been following us today. Otherwise, how did they know where you were?'

'And if they were following us,' Jackie said, 'then they must have suspected that I had something belonging to them. And that could only be something Bukanov had put in my rucksack.'

'You must be careful, Jackie,' Sean said earnestly. 'I'm ... I'm sorry I got you involved in all of this.'

'But you didn't,' she said. 'I was involved from the beginning. Whatever Bukanov put in my rucksack has dragged me into this. So it's not your fault.'

'OK,' Sean said. 'But promise me you won't take any risks.'

Jackie smiled. 'I promise,' she said. 'And the same goes for you. If these are the same people who've taken your father, then you could be in danger.'

Sean nodded. 'I'll be careful,' he said. He was silent for a moment. 'I suppose we'll go back to Dublin tomorrow as planned?' he added, his voice despondent.

'I suppose so,' Jackie said reluctantly. 'I can't see how we can get onto the island without being seen. And even if we did manage it, we'd never get into the castle. But I'm not giving up,' she added with conviction. 'I'm going to ask my Dad to make some inquiries. He's busy this week but he could come to Oldport at the weekend and tell the gardaí about our suspicions. They'd be more likely to listen to him.'

'Thanks,' Sean said. 'I appreciate it.'

'Right,' Jackie said. 'Let's get back to Granddad's.'

She had spoken optimistically, but in reality felt that they had lost their best chance of solving the mystery. Whatever Bukanov had hidden in her rucksack – if he had hidden anything – was gone. And it was unlikely that even if her father agreed to speak to the gardaí at Oldport, it would make any difference. But she had wanted to give Sean some small sliver of hope. It was the best she could do for him now.

FIFTEEN

Denis Gunne had lost all sense of time and didn't know whether it was day or night. When he held his hand before his face it was just a faint blur. The darkness was almost total. He couldn't lie down properly and only slept in fits and starts. This had added greatly to his disorientation.

He'd had no contact with anyone since Costello had visited him and his toilet bucket had last been emptied. Food was provided in a metal bowl which was thrust through a locked flap fitted in the bottom of the door. The flap opened with a screech of un-oiled hinges that set his teeth on edge.

At first he hadn't felt hungry and ignored the food, which smelled like stew. He drank bottled water that grew tepid in the stifling heat. Eventually, hunger drove him to eat, and he devoured the next meal: a bowl of cereal and three slices of dry bread.

He guessed that it was breakfast, but couldn't be sure. Costello might be trying to disorientate him by serving his meals at inappropriate times. So what appeared to be his breakfast could actually be his supper. And for all he knew, it might now be the middle of the night.

It was then that despair began to eat at him. He knew that this was not a good sign – he needed to focus even on the meals – but at times the feeling almost overwhelmed him.

He imagined he heard voices. Nightmares plagued his fitful sleep. Waking in the darkness, he thought that the nightmares were real and that whatever monster had been part of the dreams was crouched in the dark beside him. So certain was he of this, that sometimes he was convinced that he could sense its foetid breath on his face.

Terror gripped him and he scrabbled in the darkness, seeking whatever horror shared the cell with him. But the space was so small that nothing larger than a dog could have joined him.

Now, waking from one such nightmare, he lay crouched in a foetal position on the stone floor. He thrust his face into the crook of his elbow in an effort to block out the stench from the toilet bucket.

When he was awake, he tried to focus his mind on Sean and Liam and what they must be enduring. He desperately wanted to see them again, to potter in the garden with Liam or go fishing with Sean. He knew his time with Liam was limited and that was the hardest of all to bear.

He could give in, accept Costello's terms, and get out of the hole. But that would be to betray Sergei Bukanov who, at Gunne's insistence, had risked his life to try and gain freedom for them both. He owed a debt to Bukanov and he would thwart Costello until he offered him some concessions.

He knew how ruthless Hawk's people could be. He suspected that Costello had driven Bukanov to his death. And he knew that at some point Costello would give him a stark choice: work or die. When that time came, he would choose life. But until then he would continue his protest. When Costello agreed to contact Sean and Liam, then Gunne would agree to co-operate. And he clung to the hope that someone somewhere had the CD and that it would come to light and end this horror.

He must have dozed, for a noise at the door disturbed him. He expected that it was food, though even in his confused state, he was certain that only a little time had elapsed since he had last eaten. But there was no screeching sound as the flap opened, only the unmistakable noise of the key turning in the lock.

The glare of light from outside was like a physical blow and he shrank from it, raising his hand to shade his eyes and turning his face away. A shoe prodded him in the ribs. When he didn't respond he was kicked sharply on the thigh bone. There was little flesh to cushion the blow, and he gasped in pain.

'You live like a pig.' It was Costello's voice.

Why had he come? Was he going to contact Liam and Sean?

Or had he come to give him an ultimatum? What if there was no second chance?

Tendrils of fear moved in his stomach. Perhaps he had been a fool to have challenged them. They had almost certainly driven Bukanov to his death. A second death wouldn't bother their consciences.

'Here,' Costello said. 'See what I've got.'

Another kick drew a second gasp of pain. Gunne risked opening one eye, squinting against the searing light. He turned his head and saw Costello's blurred figure above him. In his hand Costello held a shiny object that reflected light in a myriad of colours.

'Recognise it?' Costello's toe struck the thigh bone with unerring accuracy.

His eyes becoming used to the light, Gunne could see the silver disk that Costello held in his hand. It was a CD. And now he recognised the handwritten label. This was the disk he had given Bukanov. His heart sank.

'You recognise it?' Costello said. 'I thought you would. So you must realise now that there's no hope left. No one's coming to save you. You'll rot here in this hole if you don't agree to co-operate and you'll never see your family again.'

He put his hand in his pocket and removed a pliers. With it he snapped the CD into pieces and threw the bits at Gunne. Then he laughed. 'I'll give you another few hours in the hole to consider things,' he went on. 'If you still refuse to co-operate – well, let's say you'll wish you had. If you think this was a shock, then wait until you see the next shock I'm planning for you.'

Costello withdrew, closing the door and locking it. The darkness gathered about Denis Gunne like a shroud. Sobs of rage and impotence and despair overwhelmed him. He wrapped his arms about his head and felt the damp of tears on his cheeks.

SIXTEEN

B uoyed up at finding the CD the previous day, on Thursday morning Costello was feeling optimistic for the first time since Bukanov's escape. But his optimism was quickly dented when Gunne still refused to co-operate. Leaving the stricken man in the black hole, Costello returned to the control centre. Here, a report from Granger awaited him.

Granger had been given the task of watching Peter Howley's house and following Jackie or Sean Gunne if they left. Costello now learned that both had gone to Oldport station and taken the train to Dublin.

Costello sat quietly for a moment. Perhaps it was time to set in motion his contingency plan for obtaining Gunne's co-operation. He had already cleared this with Hawk, who, clearly distracted by the recent events, had given the go ahead right away.

Deciding to act, Costello summoned Corridan. 'Sean Gunne has returned to Dublin,' he said. 'Take Jordan with you and bring him here. It's the only way to get his father to co-operate. And I need to find out what he and the girl know.'

'You think it's wise?' Corridan asked. 'It might bring the police down on us.'

'Not if we do it my way,' Costello said. 'Get to the grandfather while the boy's not there. From what I've read in the paper, he's a bit senile, which is a stroke of luck for us. He won't be sharp enough to see through the lies. So give him the impression that you've been sent by Doctor Gunne to take Sean to see him in London; that Gunne couldn't come to Dublin for fear of arrest. This way, no one will suspect the boy's been abducted. They'll simply think he's with his father. Use the same story on the boy. If he doesn't fall for it, take him by force.'

'What about getting him to write a note?' Corridan asked.

'No,' Costello said. 'But I will get an email sent tomorrow from London to cover our tracks. Now take an unmarked van from the mainland warehouse and do nothing to arouse suspicion. Keep me posted and make no mistakes. There have been too many already.'

+   +   +

Corridan and Jordan took a box van from the warehouse as ordered, and drove to Dublin. Here they kept watch on their target. In the afternoon, Sean Gunne emerged from the house, but went only as far as the shops. Shortly after he returned, he left again. Corridan and Jordan trailed him to Jackie's house and from there to Sean's own house. Ten minutes later, Sean and Jackie took Liam to the park.

Corridan and Jordan drove back to the grandfather's house. They parked outside and walked up to the door and rang the bell. The old man answered. 'We've been sent by your son, Denis,' Corridan told him. 'He's in trouble and can't come back home from London. He's emigrating to Australia and wants to see Sean before he goes. He's sent us to collect him. So he'll be away for a while.'

'But he'll keep in touch. OK?' Jordan said.

The old man looked shocked and confused as his eyes flicked from one speaker to the other. 'What?' he said, reaching for the doorjamb to steady himself. 'What?' he called again, as they turned about and walked down the path to the gate.

'Your plan should work out fine,' Corridan told Costello when he rang him from the van after the old man had gone back inside. 'The grandfather's not completely gaga, but we gave him such a shock that I'd say he's fallen for our story.'

'Good,' Costello said. 'Tomorrow's email will clinch it. The police'll assume that the boy has gone to his father. Even if they are suspicious, they'll be looking in the wrong place. Now don't slip up. And let me know as soon as you have the boy.'

Corridan and Jordan waited in the van for their prey to return. They were men who were used to waiting and they sat patiently, the radio on low.

+   +   +

Sean's bus dropped him on the main road and he walked from there. As he passed the local takeaway, the smell of chips and burgers stimulated his taste buds. His grandfather liked cod and chips and Sean called him on the mobile to see if he should bring some back.

'These men came here in a van,' his grandfather began straight away in a querulous voice. 'They ... they said Denis sent them. They ...' The old man's voice broke.

Sean clutched the phone tighter. His heart was fluttering and he had a light feeling in the pit of his stomach.

'What's that, Granddad?' he said, trying to sound calm. 'Did you say that my dad sent them?'

'He's ... he's going to Australia,' the old man said. 'I thought he'd come and see me. I ...' His voice trailed off, sadness and confusion mingled with his words.

Sean was thinking fast. Could the men have come from his father? It seemed unlikely. And his dad would never abandon Liam to go to Australia. So the men had to be lying.

But what did they want with him? Sean wondered. Did they not find what they were looking for in Jackie's rucksack? Did they think he might have it? Whoever had driven Bukanov to his death had been desperate. And if they were the same people behind the theft of the rucksack, then they must still be desperate to have shown themselves to his grandfather, even if he were somewhat senile. That meant they mustn't have found what they were looking for and assumed he must have it. He would have to be very careful.

'Granddad,' Sean said now. 'Are those men there with you?'

'No,' his grandfather said. 'No one's here.'

'Right,' Sean said. 'I'm going to hang up now. If those men call again, don't tell them I've phoned. Say you haven't heard from me.'

'But aren't you talking to me now,' the old man said.

There was no point trying to explain, Sean realised. He would only upset his grandfather even more. Most of the time he understood what was happening. But whenever he became upset or excited, he tended to become confused.

'Bye for now, Granddad,' Sean said and he cut the connection, angry and sad at the same time. He slipped the mobile in his pocket and walked on.

He turned into Sycamore Road, a tree-lined avenue that ran parallel to Orchard Road. An alleyway linked both roads and he made his way through to the end. From there he could see his grandfather's house. There was a van parked outside. It was a small unmarked box van with a roller shutter rear door and separate cab.

An idea was taking shape in his mind. He realised that it could be dangerous but it was too good a chance to miss. Coming to a decision, he retreated up the alleyway, took out his mobile and called his grandfather's sister, Eileen. When she answered, he asked her if she could come over and spend the night with her brother, something she did on occasions. 'I'm going to stay the night with friends,' he lied. 'I should be back sometime tomorrow.'

The old lady grumbled as usual but eventually agreed, and to Sean's relief asked no awkward questions. Sean then dialled his grandfather's house, imagining him waiting by the phone for it to ring. 'It's Sean, Granddad,' he said. 'I'm afraid I won't be home tonight. So I've arranged for Eileen to come over and stay with you. OK? Now, could you ask the men who are waiting outside in the van to come in and speak to me.'

'You're not coming home?' His grandfather sounded upset.

'I can't, Granddad,' Sean said patiently. 'But Eileen will come over to be with you. Now please go out and ask those men to come in. And don't hang up the phone, all right? I want to speak with them.'

'You want to speak with them. I'll tell them that.'

Sean heard a clatter as the phone was put down. He crept to the end of the alleyway and watched the house. Moments later the door opened and he saw his grandfather make his way unsteadily down the path to the waiting van.

He heard a mumbled conversation but was too far away to make out what was said. He held his breath, hoping his ruse would work. If neither of the men got out, or only one did so, then his plan wouldn't work.

To his relief, both got out, slamming the doors shut. He waited until the front door closed, then he moved out of the alleyway and strode briskly towards the van. He took shelter behind a tree from where he could see the front door, but where anyone emerging from the house couldn't see him. He held the mobile to his ear and heard the clatter of the receiver as it was picked up in the house.

'Yeah?' A man spoke.

'Where's my dad?' Sean asked, not needing to feign anxiety.

'Who's this?'

'Sean Gunne. Now tell me where's my father?' As he spoke, Sean stepped out from behind the tree and walked towards the van. He felt exposed and uncertain, his heart still pounding in his chest.

'I can't say anything over the phone,' the man said. He had an American accent but wasn't the man Sean had spoken to the night his father disappeared.

'Look, I want to know,' Sean said, playing for time. He reached the rear of the van and stooped to examine the shutter lock. There was a gap between the shutter and the van floor. It wasn't fully closed. Sean held his breath, frightened that his relief might be evident over the line.

'I can't tell you,' the man said. He sounded angry and impatient. 'It's too dangerous. But I can tell you he's fine and waiting to see you. Only we haven't much time. Every second you delay us puts his life in danger. I will explain everything to you on the way.'

'I want to know *now*,' Sean insisted. He glanced towards the house. The door was still closed. There was no sign of activity within. Sean pressed the mute button on the phone and pushed the shutter up about a metre. In his ear he heard the man repeating almost word for word what he had already said.

The van held cardboard boxes, stacked on either side of a central aisle. In the light from the street lamp Sean could see that the rows of boxes didn't extend fully to the front of the van. Satisfied, he released the mute button and raised the phone to his ear. 'Tell me where my dad is,' he said, 'and I'll come and meet you.'

'I can't do that,' the man shouted. 'Don't you realise this phone is probably tapped. You want the cops to get him?'

'I'm not coming back,' Sean said, ignoring this. 'I'm going to Oldport. I think my dad's there and I'm going to find him.'

The sharp intake of breath told him that he had struck the right note. There was muffled whispering before the man spoke. 'Oldport?' he said. 'Never heard of it.'

'It's where that man was killed by the train,' Sean said. 'I think that's where the drug pushers are holding my father. I think he's a prisoner there and I'm going to find him.'

He cut the connection, switched off the phone, and slipped beneath the shutter into the van. Once inside, he pushed the shutter closed, leaving a gap of a few centimetres. The glimmer of light that came through the gap and from some vents in the roof provided the only relief from the darkness.

Sean felt his way up the aisle to the top of the van. Folded up in a corner of the cavity formed by the boxes was a mattress from a camp bed. It confirmed, if he needed confirmation, that the men had intended abducting him and hiding him here. If they re-stacked the boxes to block the central aisle, only a thorough search would find him.

Sean sat on the mattress, awaiting the return of his attempted abductors. If they checked the van, then the game was up. But if not, he would find out where his father was when they reached their destination, which he felt certain must be Oldport.

He heard the men coming back and held his breath. They climbed into the cab and drove off immediately. The roar of the engine made it impossible for him to hear if they were speaking.

All he could do now was await developments. He knew he should have called someone to explain what he was doing. But he didn't have time. He considered ringing Jackie, but what could she do? It was too late to talk him out of it, so she would almost certainly contact the gardaí. That would ruin everything.

Committed now, Sean unfolded the mattress and lay down.

If they were heading for Oldport, then he knew he had some long, uncomfortable hours to endure. But if it meant finding his father, then it would be worth it.

+ + +

While Jordan drove, Corridan contacted Costello on his mobile. 'You've messed up,' Costello shouted, clearly furious. 'Can't I trust you to do anything right?'

'It's not our fault,' Corridan said defensively. 'Anyway, our target is on his way to Oldport. We can pick him up there.'

'No names,' Costello screamed. 'Don't you understand basic security? Now get back here right away.'

'We'll need to eat,' Corridan protested.

'Eat on the move then,' Costello spat. 'I want you back here in four hours.'

The line went dead. Corridan swore as he pocketed the phone. When he got his hands on the Gunne boy, he'd make him suffer. And he *would* get his hands on him. The inevitable had merely been postponed.

SEVENTEEN

Sean knew they had left the city when their speed increased and the orange glow from the vents faded. For the time being he could relax. He settled himself more comfortably on the mattress, and eventually sleep claimed him.

When he awoke, he thought he was at home in his own bed. But that didn't explain the cold or the discomfort he felt. Then reality poured in upon him and he jerked upright, listening.

There was no engine noise. They had stopped. He cocked his ear and heard muffled voices. They came from the cab of the vehicle but he couldn't make out what they said.

Were they in Oldport, he wondered? Or had they stopped somewhere along the way? Or was he completely mistaken in his conclusions and were they in some other place entirely? But those questions would soon be answered. What mattered now was not to be discovered, nor let the two men out of his sight.

The van rocked as the men got out. Two doors slammed and he heard fading footsteps. Silence enveloped him. He listened intently but no sound broke the quiet. His eyes adjusted to the darkness and he held his watch up to his face. He could just make out the dial – it was 1am.

He scrambled to his feet, muscles aching, and tiptoed to the rear door. Again he listened. Nothing. All was hushed. It was difficult to imagine there was danger out there. But he dared not relax his vigilance for a single moment.

He eased the shutter up a little and peered out. The van was parked in what looked like an industrial estate with rows of warehouses facing onto a central, poorly lit road. To his right, a steel gate set in a high chain link fence, and giving access to another poorly lit road, was closing automatically; someone had obviously just gone outside.

He didn't know where he was. It might be Oldport, but then again it could be anywhere. The journey had taken nearly four hours: the time it would take to reach Oldport from Dublin. So the odds on him being in Oldport were quite good.

His priority now was to get out of the industrial estate. But the fence and gate formed a formidable barrier. The gate was obviously operated by either a remote control or a code, neither of which he possessed. The only way out was to scale it.

He had not heard a vehicle, so that meant that his would-be abductors had left on foot. They couldn't be too far away. If he could scale the gate quickly, he should be able to catch sight of them before they disappeared, and follow them.

He ran to the gate and, without even stopping to consider whether it was alarmed or not, grabbed the steel bars and began to climb. To his relief, it was much easier than he could have imagined. There were no shortage of handholds and footholds. Clearly the gate was primarily intended to prevent vehicles illegally entering or leaving the estate.

Once safely on the other side, Sean peered around the concrete pier on which the gate hung. On his right, the road ended at a second steel gate which gave access to another industrial estate.

On his left, the road ran downhill, lined on both sides by small houses, many of which were boarded up. A few vehicles were parked along the pavements, but the area had an air of neglect about it. Sean scanned the vicinity for the two men, but there was no sign of them. They had disappeared.

Bitterly disappointed, he set off downhill, certain that they must have gone in that direction. At the bottom of the hill he came to a junction and, exercising caution, peered around the corner in both direction. There was still no sign of the two men. But he recognised the street. He was in Oldport. He *had* been right. Oldport held the key to his father's disappearance and to Bukanov's death. Or rather Fair Island did. He was certain of that now.

There was no sign of his quarry, but he assumed that they were headed for the jetty and a boat back to the island. If he turned left, and left again at the next junction, it would take him down to the jetty. But how could he reach the island? He thought about borrowing an inflatable from Peter Howley's boat and rowing there. But the idea of venturing out to sea alone in the dark was daunting.

The fast food place where he had gone with Jackie after her rucksack was stolen was about twenty metres further along the street on his right. He could smell the chips and realised he was hungry. But food would have to wait

He turned left and walked down to the next junction and turned left again. The street was deserted and he walked warily to the end. Peering around the corner, he saw the jetty and, beyond it, the anchored boats. 'Spirit of Abraham', which he had seen at the jetty on Fair Island, was tied up at the jetty here, its lights glowing in the darkness.

As he watched, a man emerged from the cabin of the boat. Sean shrank back into a shop doorway as the man stared directly towards him. But he quickly realised that the man couldn't see him. He was looking beyond Sean, as if seeking someone.

Only now did it strike Sean that the two men from the van hadn't yet reached the jetty. That must mean that they were no longer ahead of him, but behind him. For all he knew, they were heading this way right now. He was trapped between them and the man on the boat.

How much time did he have? Time enough to reach the side street and take cover there? He hesitated, uncertain. And when he looked out again, it was too late. The two men were coming towards him.

If he ran now he would give himself away. They would rec-ognise him and give chase. They could easily take him in this deserted place.

He remembered what Jackie had said about the fear she had

seen in Bukanov's eyes. They had hunted Bukanov down, just as they would hunt him down.

The recess where he hid was very shallow. He stood on tiptoe, as if doing so would make him thinner, and shrunk back into the corner. Hands pressed to his side, he held his breath, not daring to blink an eye.

He heard them approach. They were talking together, but he shut his ears to their words. Their footsteps seemed loud and ominous.

If only someone would come along ... But no other footsteps or voices broke the silence. There was nothing now but the men's voices and their footsteps and the thump, thump, thump of his heart.

He could smell chips as they approached, almost taste the tangy vinegar on his tongue. Metre by metre they drew closer. A street lamp cast their shadows before them and his first glimpse was of their ghostly shapes floating on the pavement.

Then they were there, side by side, passing him by, so close that he could reach out and touch them. He clenched his eyes shut, certain that even that movement made a whisper of sound. Then he gingerly opened one eye. As if that were a signal, the voices and the footsteps stopped. Silence stretched like a too tight violin string; the slightest movement or sound would snap it.

Run, his instincts told him. But fear held his feet firmly on the ground. Then it was too late. They had turned back and their dark, looming shapes filled the doorway.

He made a desperate attempt to escape, diving low between them. He almost made it – was almost through when hands grabbed him and held him. He opened his mouth to shout for help.

A clenched fist struck him sharply on the side of the head. He grunted from the impact of the blow and the surge of pain. Lights flashed before his eyes. Then another blow struck him and he found himself falling down into a deep, bottomless pit.

EIGHTEEN

When Sean came to, he found the whole world swinging on a string. Nausea welled up in his throat and he had to fight it. He moved his head and a darting pain made him gasp. It brought him back to reality and he knew where he was: on the boat to Fair Island. It was where he'd wanted to go, but not as a prisoner.

He opened his eyes. Harsh light seared his eyeballs and he shut them again. Tentatively he re-opened them, turning his head away from the strip light fitted in the ceiling. He was in the boat's galley, curled up on the floor like a caterpillar. To his surprise he was not tied up, but then there was little hope of escape. There was no place to go except overboard and there the sea would soon claim him.

He had behaved foolishly, but it was too late for recriminations. He should have let someone know what was happening. And maybe it wasn't too late. Hoping against hope, he searched his pocket for his mobile phone. It wasn't there.

He could hear men's voices outside, but not what they were saying. Slowly he got to his feet, pain and nausea making him unsteady. He held onto a worktop until his balance returned.

Then he tried the handle of the galley door. It was locked.

Resigned to his fate, he waited. The boat slowed and then bumped gently to a stop. The engines were cut. The boat rocked gently in the swell and he heard muffled voices again.

Someone unlocked the galley door. It was one of the men from the van. 'Let's go,' the man said. Sean followed him up on deck and onto the jetty where the second man waited. He immediately recognised the floodlit complex nearby. He was on Fair Island.

The men bundled him into the rear of a waiting jeep, then got in the front themselves. They drove off at high speed. No one spoke.

Within minutes, they entered the castle complex through automatic gates in the chain link fence. Sean heard them clang shut behind them. The thought struck him that he might never escape, never again see Liam or his mother or his grandfather.

They drove through an archway into a large courtyard and stopped by the entrance to the main tower. Sean was manhandled from the jeep and escorted into the tower. He had time to note that the courtyard was enclosed on all sides by buildings; the only exit was through the archway.

They passed through a massive oak door into a large, dimly lit flag stoned hall. The walls were of dark stone and windowless. Their footsteps echoed as they crossed the floor towards a glassed-off area which extended the full width of the hall. Dotted about the hall stood suits of armour. Weapons from another time – swords and spears and axes – hung on the walls.

In contrast, the glassed-off area was bright, carpeted and filled with high tech equipment. A number of monitors fixed to one wall showed the grainy black and white pictures of surveillance cameras. There were other banks of control panels and switches and digital readouts and a large radio transceiver. Two doors led off the room, both at the rear.

A man in the uniform of a security guard sat behind a large desk on which there was a computer monitor and keyboard and a number of telephones. Another man was perched on the edge of the desk, dressed in a woollen robe and leather slippers. His blonde hair was cut close to his skull. His face was stark, almost blank, the eyes as cold and as dead as those of a frozen salmon. Sean couldn't help but shiver.

'Well, what have we here?' The robed man had an American accent. He could have been the man who had answered Sean's call the night his father disappeared. But Sean couldn't be certain. 'So you've come to visit us at last.' The man snorted and the other men laughed. But there was no humour in their laughter.

'I want to see my father,' Sean said. He kept his voice neutral, not making his words a demand.

The man stared at him quizzically. 'Your father?' he said. 'Who would he be?'

'Denis Gunne,' Sean said. 'Doctor Denis Gunne.'

'What if we never heard of him?'

'They did,' Sean said, pointing to his abductors. 'They told me a story about taking me to see him tonight. Only I fooled them.'

The man who'd struck him in Oldport raised his hand as if to strike again. 'Corridan.' The robed man spoke quietly. Corridan withdrew his hand as if it had been burnt. 'Right,' the robed man continued. 'You're a smart-ass, are you? Well we have ways of dealing with smart-asses here.'

'What are you going to do?' Sean demanded defiantly. 'Are you going to deal with me like you dealt with Sergei Bukanov?'

The name silenced them. The robed man narrowed his eyes. But his expression never altered. 'I'm Costello,' he said, very quietly. 'There are questions I want answered. You may decide to play the smart-ass, but let me assure you that if you do, then in a few minutes you'll be begging to answer. Do you understand?'

Sean didn't respond. He tried to look defiant but fear gripped him with icy fingers. He knew he was at the mercy of these men. He had already witnessed Corridan's brutal violence, but it was this quietly spoken man he feared the most.

'Do you understand?' Costello repeated.

'I have nothing to say,' Sean said. 'Now I want my father and myself taken to the mainland.'

Costello's expression never altered. 'When you've satisfactorily answered my questions,' he said, 'then you can make a request. Now, who told you that your father was here on Fair Island?'

'I want my father and myself taken to the mainland,' Sean repeated. 'When we're safely there, I'll answer your questions.'

He knew it was a dangerous gamble. These men were in control and could do to him whatever they wished. No one knew he was here. Even when Jackie learned that he had disappeared, who would believe her story about Fair Island? And it was very likely that, in the circumstances, his grandfather would get the whole story mixed up and confuse everybody.

But despite knowing this and, aware of the power that these men held over him, Sean still wanted to test them – to call their bluff. It was unlikely that Costello would harm him until he'd learned how Sean had known about Fair Island and who he might have told. So Sean felt that he might be able to bargain with Costello. It was worth trying, until he was threatened with real danger, and then the sensible thing to do would be to give in.

'I'll give you one more chance,' Costello said. 'Now answer my question.'

Sean remained silent. He stared at the floor, refusing to acknowledge Costello's presence. 'You've had your chance,' Costello said. 'Now we'll try another method.' He rose. 'Come quietly,' he added, 'or be dragged along by the hair. It's your choice.'

'Where are you taking me?' Sean asked.

'You'll see,' Costello said. 'Corridan,' he ordered. 'Bring him along.'

Sean caught a whiff of aftershave as Costello left the control room through the door on the left. As he did so, Corridan struck Sean across the head with his open hand. It was a slight blow, but delivered with such speed that it stunned him. Then he was grabbed roughly by the collar of his jacket and frog-marched after Costello.

He found himself in another section of the tower. Here a metal stairs led downwards. A steel gate blocked the flight at the bottom. Beside the stairs there was a large lift. But before his mind could register anything else, Corridan almost threw him down the stairs. The gate at the bottom opened automatically in response to a code that Costello punched into a keypad mounted on the wall.

As they passed through, Sean noted that the keypad had a tiny built-in screen; it showed a row of asterisks, like the ones that came up on his computer screen when he logged in his password. They obviously corresponded to the code.

He was aware of two corridors branching off at right angles and a door beside the lift which resembled the time-locked door to a bank vault. He was also aware of the loud humming of electric motors.

Costello took the corridor to the left. Corridan pushed Sean so that he stumbled after Costello. A metre further on there was a stone spiral stairs, blocked with another steel gate. Doors opened off the corridor on both sides. Through one, Sean glimpsed what looked like a laboratory.

He was marched along the corridor and through an archway into a much darker and more dismal part of the dungeons. Here, the stone walls were damp and showing the ravages of time. Sean's fear grew until he was in the grip of terror. His legs wobbled and threatened not to support him. He was certain that he would have fallen if Corridan hadn't gripped his jacket and supported him.

Sean's imagination began to run riot. He pictured the place with iron chains and shackles fixed to the walls – a torture chamber where blazing fires heated iron instruments until they glowed white-hot in the coals. Already he could smell the stench of scorched flesh and hear the screams of helpless victims.

His fear was a physical thing; it weighed him down and he felt on the verge of collapse. All his earlier resolve weakened and he wanted to scream out that he would do whatever they asked, answer any questions they might have. His mind became filled with images of the horrors awaiting him so that he was prepared for anything. Or so he believed.

They crossed the uneven stone floor to a recess lit by a single bulb. Here a low steel door was fitted. A stench hung in the damp air. Sean saw Costello clamp a hand over his mouth and nose. Corridan pushed past Sean and, turning his face aside, unlocked the steel door with a heavy key that hung on a hook on the wall. Then he swung the door open on creaking hinges.

A foul stench burst from the dark hole beyond the door and Sean thought he was going to be thrown into a cesspool. He clamped his fingers to his nose and turned away and retched. Bile burned his throat.

Costello caught his shoulder with his free hand. His grip was powerful and it forced Sean to turn back towards that dark cavity. 'Look,' Costello ordered. There was a crumpled form on the floor.

Costello thrust Sean further forward. Close up he could see that it was a man, curled up in a foetal position, facing the back wall. His hands and arms were wound around his head as if to ward off an attack.

The space, a hole cut in rock, was tiny. The man could not stretch out fully nor stand upright. There was no ventilation or natural light and even out in the open the stench of human waste was overpowering. What it must be like in that confined space when the door was closed, Sean could not imagine.

He knew why he was being shown this prisoner. This was what awaited him if he did not comply with Costello's requests. He would be given a choice now: tell Costello what he knew or end up in the hole.

But Costello did not make any threats. Instead he nodded to Corridan who stepped forward and prodded the crumpled form with his shoe. The man whimpered but did not move. Corridan kicked him sharply and viciously in the kidneys, drawing a grunt of pain.

'No, please ...' Sean managed to gasp. He couldn't bear to be the cause of any more suffering to the poor wretch.

Corridan ignored his plea and kicked the helpless man again. 'Turn around,' he ordered. 'Turn around.'

Sean watched helplessly as the crumpled figure stirred and slowly turned his upper body towards them. His hands and arms still protected his head and face but part of his features were visible. Stubble grew on the exposed flesh, giving his face a dark wild look. His dark hair was dirty and matted.

Sean stared down at the face as bile rose again in his throat. He closed his eyes and opened them. But the reality didn't change. He screamed and tried to throw himself at the figure. Costello caught him in a vice-like grip.

'Nooo!' Sean's scream echoed back off the walls. The man on the floor was his father.

NINETEEN

'You will tell me everything,' Costello said quietly when they returned to the control centre. 'Otherwise your father stays where he is.'

'Please,' Sean said, on the verge of despair. 'Let him out and I'll tell you anything you want. Please ...'

'Just tell me,' Costello repeated in his cold voice. 'I will not ask you again.'

Sean knew that if he were to help his father he had to do as Costello ordered. Near to tears and in a stumbling voice, he recounted how that chance remark about Doctor Dolittle had led him to think that Bukanov had been with his father. Then, when he learned that Bukanov had been a champion swimmer, he had thought that he might have swum from Fair Island.

'That was why I came to Oldport,' Sean said. 'I wanted to find out what I could.'

'And what did you find out?' Costello asked.

'Nothing,' Sean said. 'I didn't find out anything. I thought I'd been mistaken and I went back to Dublin.' As he spoke he began to get a grip on himself. He was coming to realise that he and his father were not the only ones in danger. Jackie would be in trouble too if Costello suspected she knew anything.

'When those men called on Granddad, claiming to come from my father,' Sean went on, 'I became suspicious. So I decided to hide in the van and see where they went.' He shrugged his shoulders as if to say the rest was obvious.

Costello then questioned him about Jackie and here Sean lied. 'We're kind of ... well friends,' he mumbled. 'We go to the same school and ...' He trailed off as if he were embarrassed.

Costello interrogated him further, going over and over what Sean had already told him. Sean stuck to his story, which was true except for knowing Jackie, and eventually Costello seemed satisfied. He asked Sean who knew what he had planned, and here again Sean stuck to the truth. 'I couldn't tell anyone,' he pointed out. 'Not even Jackie. If I did, they would have tried to stop me.'

Costello sat quietly for some moments. 'Right,' he said eventually to Corridan. 'Take him down.'

'But my dad,' Sean protested. 'I ... I want to see him – to talk to him.'

'Take him,' Costello said, turning away.

Sean was dragged back down the stairs and locked in a small room off the main corridor. Rage, sadness and despair gripped him and he threw himself on the bed.

He tried desperately to black out the pitiful image of his father, but that wretched face and the sound of his pain as Corridan kicked him were etched in his mind. Face down on the bed, his face buried in the pillow, he felt tears behind his eyes. An obstruction lodged in his throat.

But he was determined not to cry, or give in to self-pity. His father was fighting them and so would he. He vowed that Costello would never hold them. They would escape, and tell the world of their abduction and Bukanov's death. They would see Costello and Hawk Silvermann locked away forever. That would be the dream that would sustain him, Sean vowed, no matter what happened.

Now he realised just how stupid it had been not to tell anyone where he was going. Why hadn't he phoned Jackie or Liam last night? It would have made all the difference. They would know where he was and could get help. But it was too late for that now.

It was warm and the constant hum of the motors irritated him. But eventually sleep claimed him. In his dreams he saw his father, prison bars casting dark vertical shadows on him. Sean reached through the bars and tried to catch his father's hand. But he was out of reach. Someone shook him and he woke. Costello was staring down at him. 'Mr Silvermann wants to see you,' Costello said.

'I must see my father first,' Sean said.

'Let me explain something,' Costello said, his voice laced with venom. 'When I say jump, you jump. I'm in charge here. I can keep your father in the hole as long as I wish. His freedom from that hell is in your hands now. Do you want to see him rot there? It's your decision. I won't speak of this again. From now on, when I give an order you obey immediately. Right?'

'Yes.' Sean nodded to emphasise his acquiescence. 'But,' he added, 'I don't understand what you want my father to do.'

'Mr Silvermann will explain everything,' Costello said. 'Come on. You're keeping him waiting and he is not a patient man.'

Costello took him up to the tower in the lift, punching in a code on a keypad to open the doors. Sean noted eight asterisks on the screen, each one corresponding to a letter or number of the code.

When they emerged from the lift, a large man awaited them,

silent and forbidding in his dark suit. He didn't speak or acknowledge them, but turned and walked down the flag-stoned corridor to stand at an open door. 'That's Quigly.' Costello said. 'He's deaf and dumb and as dangerous as a cornered rat. If he ever feels you're a threat to Mr Silvermann, he'll snap your neck like a twig.'

It was not a threat, just a statement of fact. Sean shivered as Costello ushered him through the open door into a study which resembled a smaller version of the control centre. Here they were confronted by a man in a powered wheelchair who sat behind a large desk.

'Leave us,' the man said. Costello withdrew, closing the door behind him.

'Sit.' The man indicated a leather swivel chair.

From where he sat, Sean could see a gold-framed picture on the desk. In it was a photograph of a smiling boy holding a baseball bat. A plaque at the bottom of the frame was engraved with a name and with two dates: Abraham Silvermann. June 24th 1991 – July 15th 2001.

'So you're Sean Gunne,' the man said. 'I'm Max Silvermann; people call me Hawk.'

Sean didn't speak.

'You met your father,' Hawk said. It was a statement. 'He has not been very co-operative. We have tried persuading him, but he is obstinate. With you here I feel he will help us in any way he can. Don't you agree?'

Sean stayed silent and he saw the other's face grow dark with anger. 'It would appear,' he said quietly, 'that Costello has not fully explained the situation. I do not repeat myself. Do you understand?'

'Yes,' Sean said, realising that silence would gain him nothing.

'Good,' Hawk said. 'Now let me show you something.' He

picked up a remote control from the desk and aimed it at a cabinet in a corner of the room. The doors of the cabinet slid back to reveal a wide-screen television and video recorder and shelves of tapes. Hawk pressed more buttons and the screen came to life. A whirring sound indicated that the video had begun to play.

It was a home movie of a party held on the lawn of an imposing white house. Men and women sat at tables beneath sunshades, while maids served food from a nearby barbecue. At two long tables, children were eating ice-cream sundaes. One laughing boy waved at the camera, his brown eyes alive with merriment and mischief. It was the boy in the photograph.

The camera panned from table to table. The women smiled and the men made mock salutes. One woman in a white dress stuck out her tongue, and there was loud laughter.

The next scene showed an expanse of green with a baseball diamond marked on it. Adults and children were in the process of playing a game. The camera followed the play, but dwelt for the most part on the boy who had earlier waved at the camera.

'That is my son, Abraham,' Hawk Silvermann said. 'On his tenth birthday. Three weeks later he was killed in a car accident.'

There was no emotion in the voice, but Sean could see that the hand holding the remote control was trembling. While Sean watched, Hawk pressed one of the buttons and the video machine whirred as it went into forward search mode. He let it run on, then brought it back to normal speed again.

Now a man was batting . It was Hawk himself. The pitcher pitched and the bat swung and the ball soared skywards. The batter began to run. Hawk paused the machine, catching himself in mid flight, frozen, immobilised.

'I was once that man you saw batting. Now I'm as helpless as the man in the freeze frame. My punishment was to survive the car crash that killed my son and my wife. But to survive as a cripple.'

'I want to walk again. I want life to go back to what it was before. And I will make it happen.' He was staring at Sean but his mind seemed elsewhere, maybe out there on that baseball diamond, bat in hand, the pitcher preparing to deliver the ball.

'My brain was damaged in the accident and it has left me without the use of my legs. But I know the injury can be repaired. With infusions of stem cells my brain can regenerate itself and give me back my mobility. I will be able to walk again and have my life back. That is why we are here.'

Hawk pressed a button on the remote and the man on the screen began to run again. 'That is what I want to achieve,' Hawk said. 'That is what I *will* achieve. Stem cell therapy will be the greatest breakthrough in the history of medicine. But the world is full of fools ...' He jabbed at the remote and the figure on the screen froze again.

There was silence for a moment. Sean stared at Hawk, some things a little clearer now. But there were so many unanswered questions.

'You wonder what all this has to do with your father?' Hawk asked. 'To realise my dream, I needed scientists. I needed to assemble a team of some of the best scientists in their fields. Your father was one of the men I wanted.'

'So it was you who tried to frame him for drug dealing,' Sean said, his voice angry and bitter. 'To force him to come to work for you. And when that didn't work, you had him abducted.'

'I had to have him,' Hawk said simply. 'Bukanov was good but he didn't have your father's brilliance.'

'But why all the secrecy?' Sean said.

'Because of the moral fools.' Hawk almost spat out the

words. 'Stem cells are harvested from living embryos, which then die. There are those who believe that an embryo is a human being and that to kill it, even for the good of others, is wrong. But that is just religious nonsense. How can a cluster of cells be a human being? And as for the belief in a soul ... That stems from man's fear of death – his desire to live forever. So these moral fools want to limit the quality of life here in return for some stupid dream of immortality in another life.'

'I know there isn't any life after death,' Hawk continued. 'But try convincing those fools who make the laws.' He thumped the desk. 'In their blind stupidity, they have made laws which limit experimentation on embryos. What is the difference between an embryo that is two weeks old and one that is four weeks old if both are not going to survive? It is this sort of nonsense that is hampering progress. I want to carry out research without these restrictions, but that is deemed either unethical or illegal, and so I cannot work openly.'

Sean had read about genetic research and the advances that were being made. And he knew that there was huge opposition from those who believed that even to experiment on day-old embryos was wrong.

'There is also much debate about whether what I intend to achieve is possible,' Hawk continued. 'I believe it is. Except I believe that for one hundred percent efficiency, one's own stem cells must be used. That is the key. One must use one's own body to cure itself.'

Hawk was becoming agitated. His hands were trembling and his eyes bulged. His breath came in raucous gasps. Sean was alarmed at the intensity of the man's emotion.

'But of course it doesn't stop at just regenerating damaged cells. I believe that we can grow our own organs – a heart, or a liver, an eye, or even a limb – using stem cells. Did you know that there are creatures that can re-grow limbs? So why not us? It would give us a second chance. We could live longer, have a better quality of life. And we could make these new organs even better than our own by manipulating the genes. Imagine my heart with the genes of an athlete?'

Hawk stopped and seemed to gain some control over his emotions. 'It will change the world,' he said. 'That is why we are here on Fair Island. That is why your father is here. I want him to help me walk again and change the world forever.'

Sean looked from the suspended figure on the television screen to the immobile man in the chair. He could understand Hawk's desire to walk again. And he could understand his determination to do anything to bring this about. But Hawk was sadly misguided if he thought he could use his own stem cells. For that he would have to be an embryo again, and that was impossible.

'You seem puzzled,' Hawk said. 'What don't you understand?'

'How can you use your own stem cells?' Sean said. He hadn't wanted to be drawn into conversation, but the man fascinated him with the fire of fanaticism that glowed in his eyes. It was what Sean imagined a zealot might look like.

'Your'e wondering how I can do such a thing – how I can harvest my stem cells? You think it's impossible, don't you? But it's not!' Hawk leaned forward, madness flaming in his eyes like a bush fire.

'Science has given me a way.' He was speaking like a man in a trance. 'With the right brains and dedication and unlimited funds, I am going to perfect the technique of human cloning. Then anyone who wishes can clone themselves and harvest the stem cells from their own embryo.'

Sean was too stunned to respond. He knew a little about cloning because he had often listened to his father speak of it, along with other developments in medicine and science. His father had not been in favour of many of the new developments. It was one of the reasons why he had given up his research career.

'What is being done will lead us all to disaster,' Sean had heard him say. 'Some things are sacred and man is crazy to meddle in them. I studied medicine to help sick people, not to play God.'

His attitude had led to a furious row with Sean's mother. 'You speak of God,' she had said one day, her voice bitter. 'Well, look at our son. Why did God allow that? What has Liam done to deserve it? And is God going to cure him?' She shook her head. 'It's science that will cure him. But it'll be too late ...' She'd run from the room then, her sobs echoing through the house.

His father had had no answer. No one had an answer. For Sean, the solution was to pray, and he had prayed every day for a miracle. 'Let Liam live,' he begged. Only now he didn't believe in miracles anymore and he knew that Liam would die.

'You have heard of cloning?' Hawk's voice brought Sean back to reality and he nodded.

'It's the perfect solution.' Hawk leaned forward. 'Scientists have cloned mammals, sheep and pigs, for example, so it is possible to clone a human being. We can clone ourselves, manipulate the genes if we wish, and harvest our own stem cells. There is no disease we won't be able to cure. Anything will be possible.'

'That is my goal. One day Fair Island will go down in history, as famous as any place where the future has been forged. When I walk, people will see what can be done and the fools and their objections will be swept away.'

'But your father is jeopardising my dream. To begin with, he wouldn't even come to Texas to discuss the matter with Herr

Brandt, the head of the research project. Then when I had him brought here, he encouraged Sergei Bukanov to escape. Now he refuses to work on the project. My patience is at an end. I cannot wait any longer. This is his final chance. I want you to persuade him to co-operate. If you achieve that, then you will be amply rewarded. But if not ...'

'I don't want your money,' Sean said, stung to anger. He hadn't intended reacting, but couldn't help it.

'I'm not talking about money,' Hawk said. 'I mean something money cannot buy. At least, not until now.'

'There's nothing I want that badly,' Sean said. 'Whether money could buy it or not.'

'Ah, but there is,' Hawk said quietly. 'Something you want more than anything on earth. And I can give it to you.'

'No.' Sean shook his head.

'No?' Hawk leaned even further forward in the chair. 'You have a brother,' he said. 'A brother who is crippled like me. A brother who will soon die.' He stopped to let his words sink in. 'I can help Liam walk again. I can play God and give him life.'

TWENTY

When Sean didn't come to the office the next morning as arranged, Jackie was annoyed. Then she began to be apprehensive. She phoned his grandfather's house and a woman answered the phone. Jackie asked to speak to Sean and the woman said that she would get Mr Gunne for her.

When Edward Gunne came on the line, Jackie asked him if she could speak to Sean. 'He's not here,' the old man said. 'He's gone away.'

'Where? Where has he gone?' Her sense of danger was much more acute now.

'I ... I don't no.'

'When did he go?' she asked.

'Last night. He ... he never came home. Now ... now I have to go.'

'Please,' Jackie pleaded, but he'd hung up. She replaced the receiver, fumbling it back in its cradle. Something had happened to Sean. He just wouldn't go off like that.

Her first thought was that they had taken Sean just like they had taken his father. Her hand was trembling as she dialled Sean's mobile. Please answer, she begged silently. But a recorded message told her that the phone was switched off or out of range.

Be calm, she told herself now. She was probably mistaken. She was allowing her imagination to run away with her. But then she remembered Sergei Bukanov, his terrified, pleading eyes and those menacing figures at either end of the platform.

Calm deserted her as she called her father. There was no answer from his phone either. She left a message asking him to call her and hung up. She switched on the answering machine and, taking her bag, locked the office and set off for the nearest bus stop.

It was then the thought struck her that she herself might be in danger. She glanced about, but everything seemed normal. People hurried by and the traffic as usual was nose to tail.

She had to run for the bus and was the last passenger to board. No one followed her on. She hurried to the rear of the bus and stared out through the back window. There was no obvious pursuit. She was safe for now and she collapsed into a seat, her heart pounding.

A second bus took her to the centre where Liam stayed while his mother was at work. As she entered, she felt foolish. There was probably a simple explanation for all of this, and Liam would have it. But when she told Liam what she knew, his face darkened. His fear matched her own. 'He wouldn't go away,' Liam said. 'Not without telling me.'

'So what do we do now?' Jackie asked. 'He could be in danger …' She stopped as she saw the distress on Liam's face.

'Let's try his mobile again,' Liam said.

Jackie followed Liam to a glass-walled office where he could use the phone. Liam dialled the number but got the same recorded message, amplified by the speaker on the desk. Liam stared at Jackie and dialled a second number. He spoke to his mother but she hadn't heard from Sean. Liam thanked her and cut the connection without any explanation.

He dialled a third number and Edward Gunne answered. Liam asked to speak to Sean. 'He's gone away,' the old man said, his voice eerily disembodied by the echo from the speaker.

'Where's he gone, Granddad?' Liam asked. 'Do you know?'

'These men called,' Edward Gunne said. His voice quivered.

Liam and Jackie exchanged apprehensive glances. 'What men?' Liam asked, keeping the anxiety out of his voice. 'Who called to the house, Granddad?'

'They … they said Denis sent them. He's emigrating to Australia. He wanted to see Sean before he went. But why wouldn't he call to see me? I … I …'

'It's all right, Granddad,' Liam soothed. 'He will come to see you. Now, when did Sean go off with these men? Do you know?'

'He ... he didn't go with them,' Edward Gunne said. 'He didn't come home. He just said he was going away. The men were angry and swore at me but it wasn't my fault.' His voice took on a childish tone.

'Don't worry about it, Granddad,' Liam said. He looked questioningly at Jackie, who shook her head to indicate that she too, was puzzled. 'So Sean didn't say where he was going?' Liam went on.

'No,' Edward Gunne said. 'He didn't say. I ... I don't know where he is.'

'Look, Granddad,' Liam said, 'you're not to worry about this. Now, is there anyone there with you?'

'My sister was here. But she's gone home now. Mrs Carroll will be calling in later.'

'I'll get my mom to call on you later too,' Liam said. 'OK?'

Liam said goodbye and hung up. His pinched face seemed more haggard and his eyes betrayed his apprehension. 'What's going on, Jackie?' he asked. 'I know something's wrong. But Sean wouldn't tell me much – only that you were investigating our father's disappearance. This has something to do with it, doesn't it?'

Jackie nodded and quietly told him all she knew. 'Do you think those men have abducted Sean and taken him to Fair Island?' he asked when she'd finished.

'I don't really know. Your Granddad said he didn't go with them.'

'That might be a ruse,' Liam said. 'If they're clever they may have wanted to give that impression. They may have forced Sean to make that call.'

Jackie nodded. It was an intelligent conclusion and she regretted now that Sean and herself hadn't taken Liam into their confidence early on. 'So what do we do now?' she asked. 'Do

130

we go to the guards or what?'

'I don't know,' Liam said. 'I don't like the fact that Sean hasn't contacted us. It would be a simple matter for him to phone and say he was OK. Even if he were out of range or hadn't got his mobile, there are phones available everywhere. So, is someone preventing him from making a call? In view of what's been happening and those men calling on Granddad, that seems the most likely explanation.'

'They must have abducted him then,' Jackie said, 'and taken him to Fair Island. But why just take Sean? I know as much as he does and I'm the one who met Sergei Bukanov. And if he did put something in my rucksack, then they've already got it. I'm certain now that it wasn't taken by mistake. So why take Sean and leave me?'

'Maybe they didn't have the opportunity,' Liam said. 'And there's no logical reason for you to disappear. If you did, there would be a hue and cry raised. But Sean *could* have gone to be with Dad. And that's exactly what the gardaí will assume if we inform them of what's happened. They won't be looking for a missing person.'

'But *why* take Sean?' Jackie insisted. 'What can they want with him?'

'I don't know,' Liam said. He shrugged helplessly.

Jackie realised that they were no nearer to solving the mystery. They didn't even know for certain if Denis Gunne had been abducted. Now they faced a similar dilemma in connection with Sean's disappearance. And they still weren't positive that Fair Island played any part in the mystery or if Sergei Bukanov's death was linked to it.

All Jackie had to rely on was her instinct, and it told her that they were linked and that Fair Island held the key. It also told her that Sean was being held there along with his father.

So where could she go from here? Liam was right: the gardaí would assume that Sean had joined his father. She didn't have the time or the facts to persuade them otherwise. She would have to do something, and do it now.

She looked at Liam. He would not hesitate to face danger to save his father or brother. Anyone with the courage to face up to his disability and the inevitability of death so young had the courage to face anything.

'We'll get Sean back,' she said quietly. 'And your father too.'

Liam nodded and reached out to grasp her hand. With that strength behind her she could do anything. She would go to Fair Island somehow. One way or another, it was time to uncover the truth.

TWENTY-ONE

Sean was in a daze when Costello took him back down from the tower. He no longer knew what to think. When Hawk had first proposed using cloned stem cells to cure his paralysis, Sean had thought him mad. But when he extended that possibility to Liam, it suddenly seemed as though the miracle he had prayed for might after all come true.

Sean was in a dilemma. What if Hawk were to succeed, and could give Liam a chance to live? Surely, as Hawk claimed, anything was justified if it was done for a good motive. And he had put forward compelling arguments to support his case.

'What is war,' Hawk had said, 'but the slaughter of human beings, most of whom are innocent? Yet we morally justify war if we see it as a struggle between good and evil. In Texas we execute murderers in the name of justice. So why then can't we clone ourselves and harvest our own stem cells to cure our illnesses? Aren't we just using our own bodies? Surely we can do what we like with them. They are ours, after all. And we're harming no one. Right now we take hearts and lungs and eyes to replace our own. But someone has to die to provide those organs. So are we not exploiting another family's tragedy, then? My way, no one dies, only a cluster of cells. Don't you agree?'

'I ... I don't know,' Sean said. 'I suppose if you don't believe in the sanctity of life it's OK. But if you believe in God, in a soul...'

'But if I clone myself, do I clone my soul too?' Hawk clenched his fists. 'Do I have a soul to clone? No one has ever proved we have a soul. So aren't we simply animals, who through some freak of evolution, have become intelligent? Isn't that really what we are: animals with the power to change our destiny? If that's so, then aren't we foolish to throw away any opportunity to make life better for ourselves?'

'Who are you to decide what is right for your brother? Isn't it his right to decide for himself? When we perfect the art of cloning here on Fair Island, doesn't your brother have the right to decide if he wants to avail of the treatment? Can you make the decision for him whether he lives or dies?'

'I ... I don't know,' Sean said.

'But you *do* know,' Hawk said. 'You know you would say yes. Anyone would. Even your father. In fact, he will do so when the time comes.'

'But won't everyone know then?' Sean said. 'You won't be able to keep it a secret. Won't you go to prison? I mean ...' He trailed off.

'For what?' Hawk said. 'The scientists in the research and development complex are working on legitimate projects, and the experts here in the castle complex who are helping me to realise my dream are running from the law or from some other fear. This is their sanctuary. They are here of their own free will. All except your father. And he will swap silence for his son's life. As for the illegal research ... when the world learns of what I have achieved, I will be feted. No one will dare speak out against me.'

'But ... but what about Sergei Bukanov?'

'He came here by choice too,' Hawk said. 'He signed an agreement to remain here like all the others. Unfortunately he was deranged and swam to the mainland and jumped in front of a train. I can't be held responsible for that, can I?'

Sean had had no answers. It seemed that Hawk had everything worked out. He knew the other scientists would keep their silence out of fear. And he believed that Sean's father would trade silence for his son's life. But even if he refused to do so, Hawk still held the upper hand. If his father didn't agree to the demands, then Hawk could simply have them both killed.

Sean couldn't banish this stark fact from his mind when Costello took him back down to his cell. Now, as he sat composing emails to be sent to his mother and Liam and Jackie, it was still there like a shadow hanging over him.

But it wouldn't come to that. His father would see that Liam's life was worth more than silence. And he himself, he knew, would do anything to give Liam a chance to live.

And that was what Hawk Silvermann was offering. 'You must

persuade your father to co-operate,' Hawk had said. 'It's your choice now.'

This burden weighed heavily on Sean. Should he try and persuade his father to work on the project and give Liam a chance for life? Or should he advise his father to refuse and let them both die? Then Liam would lose both his father and brother and still die himself. Was any principle worth that?

Hawk and Costello held all the cards. He and his father would have to comply with their wishes or face death. No one was going to come and save them. The emails he was composing would see to that. To be sent from a cyber café in London, they were part of Costello's plan to confirm the suspicion that Denis Gunne had fled rather than face prison for drug dealing. They would confirm that Sean was with him, and that they were about to make a new life for themselves elsewhere.

There would be no hue and cry raised for them. It would fit in with what the gardaí already believed. And even if his mother pressed for an investigation, the search would be concentrated in London, not on an island off the west coast of Ireland.

Sean realised that Jackie was their only hope. But only if she knew for certain that the emails were bogus and that Sean and his father were being held on Fair Island. And even if she convinced the police of this, and got them to organise a search of the island, they still might not be found.

On his return from his meeting with Hawk, Costello had shown Sean the elaborate castle security operation – the surveillance cameras, the alarms, the dogs, the coded steel doors. 'No one else will ever escape from here again,' Costello boasted. 'And even if the police come to search, we have a secret bunker.'

He had shown Sean the hidden bunker, accessed from the

library. Sean's hopes were all but dashed. They could be hidden there and no one would ever find them. But yet he was determined to get a message to Jackie to let her know where he was. It still offered some slim hope of rescue. Although, deep down he felt that if he and his father were to get away from here, they would have to plan and execute the escape themselves.

When Sean first suggested sending an email to Jackie, Costello was suspicious. 'She is my best friend,' Sean said. 'She'll think it odd if I don't contact her and let her know what's happening?'

'Write her an email then,' Costello said. 'I will decide if it can be sent. '

As Sean composed the emails, a guard brought him a bundle of clothes as Costello had promised. There were jeans and T-shirts and sweaters, a pair of sneakers as well as socks and underwear. The guard threw the clothes on the end of the bed and left without speaking.

Sean continued writing. In the emails to his mother and Liam, he wrote that he had gone to be with his father and that they were both OK. Someday soon he would get in touch with them both. He composed a similar email for Jackie, wondering how he could include some clue as to where he and his father were being held.

He knew Jackie would suspect Fair Island. So, if he could put a clue in the email, pointing towards the island, then she would know for certain that they were being held there. Maybe then she could convince her father to persuade the gardaí to carry out a thorough search of the island, and they might be found.

Sean racked his brains for some wording that would give Jackie a clue and yet would fool Costello. He would be suspicious and would refuse to send the email if he thought it contained a hidden message.

Sean glanced at the bundle of clothes. One of the sweaters, he noted, had horizontal stripes – in pink and purple! It reminded him of the jumpers his grandmother used to make for himself and Liam for Christmas. She was a whiz with the knitting needles, and as a child he had been fascinated by the way her flying fingers could weave magical patterns with the wool. As she knitted, she would explain to him the different stitches and patterns: cable stitch, crossover, plain and purl ...

Suddenly he stopped and it was as if he could hear the echo of her voice as she explained about styles and patterns. Perhaps there *was* a way after all to send a clue to Jackie. It was all Sean could do to keep his excitement under control as he wrote some final sentences on the paper Costello had provided for the purpose. 'Sorry I won't get to wear the sweater you were knitting for my birthday, Jackie. Especially after all the trouble you went to with the pattern.'

Costello came later to collect the emails. He didn't question the final sentences in the email to Jackie, nor say he would not send it. 'You're finally getting the picture,' he said. 'So I'll have a word with your father. If he agrees to Hawk's demands, I'll have him let out of the hole right away and brought up here to see you. If not, he'll stay in the hole, and you'll join him. I think he'll make the right decision. Don't you?'

Sean nodded, hoping that Costello was right. If his father agreed, then they could be together and could plan their escape. It seemed to be their only hope. While his father remained helpless in the hole, neither of them had any hope of getting out.

Did he really want his father to work on the project? Sean wondered when Costello had left. If it gave hope to Liam, shouldn't they both want it? Yet Hawk had broken the law and one man had already died because of his crazy plans. Could you justify any good that came from that evil? There was no answer to that. Sean threw himself on the bed, his mind a maelstrom of conflicting thoughts and hopes.

TWENTY-TWO

Jackie was despondent when she returned to the office after her visit to Liam. He had suggested doing nothing until he could speak with his mother. She would undoubtedly contact the police, but they, like her, would assume that Sean had gone with his father.

She had letters to type for her father but her heart wasn't in it. She typed part of one, then sat staring at the computer screen. A message flashed up saying she had email and immediately she was alert, hoping it was from Sean. She accessed her inbox. There was a single email. When she saw that the subject box contained the words: Message from Sean Gunne, she gasped aloud. With nervous fingers she opened the email and read it.

It stated that he had gone to London to be with his father. Both of them were fine and he was sending this message from a cyber café there. London – and with his father? Did that mean that everything the police suspected about Doctor Gunne was true, and that Sean knew it now? That was the implication, wasn't it? For a moment, Jackie looked at the stark statement again, a disappointed, hollow feeling in the pit of her stomach. Then she read on. 'Knitting a sweater?' What was he talking about? She couldn't cast on a stitch, never mind knit a sweater.

She stared at the words, trying to solve the puzzle. Was it a code? Maybe it contained a secret message, but she couldn't figure it out. With a sudden lift of her heart, she realised that if Sean had had to resort to a code, then the rest of the message was probably not genuine. Someone was forcing him to send it!

Was he in London? she wondered. It was possible, but she knew that anyone could have sent the email from there. She looked at the time. Liam and his mother should be home now. She picked up the telephone and dialled their number. Liam answered and she read out the email.

'I wonder if we've got one,' Liam said, his voice filled with hope. 'Let me go and check and I'll ring you back.'

He was back within minutes. 'We've got one too,' he said excitedly. 'It's similar to yours, but without the bit about the knitting. He says he's in London with Dad and will keep in contact, and we're not to worry about him.'

'The bit about the knitting doesn't make sense,' Jackie said. 'I never promised to knit a sweater for him. I don't even know when it's his birthday.'

'It was two months ago,' Liam said.

'Then it's definitely a message,' Jackie said. 'And there is a clue in it. But I can't make head or tail of it. Are you any good at crosswords or anagrams?'

'Not bad,' Liam said. 'I'll try and work it out.'

'I'll try too,' Jackie said. 'But I've never been good at this sort of thing. Now I'll read it out and you copy it.'

When that was done, Jackie inquired as to what his mother's reaction had been to Sean's disappearance. 'She's very angry,' Liam said, the hurt clear in his voice. 'She thinks that Sean has run off with Dad. She's contacted the police and told them that. Now this email will make her certain she's right.'

'So it's up to us then,' Jackie said. 'It looks like we're the only ones who can save Sean and your father.'

She rang off and printed out the email. Then she took pen and paper and wrote out the sentences in block capitals. She rearranged the words to see if she could decipher a secret message in them. She filled a page and then another page, but she could make no sense out of any of it.

Frustrated, she put it aside, having to admit defeat for the time being. But she was determined to try again. She wouldn't give up until she had exhausted every possible combination of word and letter. She would visit Liam later and they would work on it together.

+   +   +

After Costello took away the emails, Sean waited anxiously for the next development. Two hours passed. Then there was a commotion outside his cell and he rose anxiously to his feet. The cell door was unlocked and when it swung inwards, his father stood in the doorway, supported by Costello and Corridan.

Sean threw himself at the figure, and without Costello's and Corridan's support, would have knocked him down. Sean held his father, feeling the rise and fall of his chest as he breathed. His father was clean and fresh. There was no evidence of the earlier stench.

'Stand back,' Costello growled, 'so we can bring him in.'

Sean released his father, and stepped back. Costello and Corridan guided the weakened figure to the single chair. Sean hovered beside them, unable to believe that his father was here. The circumstances of their reunion didn't seem to matter just now. It was enough that they were together.

'I will have some soup brought to you,' Costello said. He

looked pointedly at Sean. 'You must convince your father to co-operate. I'll give you an hour to persuade him. If you fail, then you go down in the hole.'

He withdrew, closing the door and relocking it. Sean had imagined this moment since his father first went missing, and had often rehearsed what he would say when they finally met. But now those words had deserted him.

His father seemed older and weaker, almost like grandfather Gunne whom he resembled. Sean sat on the bed and stared at the slumped figure in the chair. Sean's spirits sank. What if they had already broken him? He had heard of such things happening and the possibility terrified him.

His father hadn't looked directly at him yet. His head was bent forward and Sean could see the first grey ribs among the dark sheen of his hair. He wanted to reach out and run his fingers through the hair, but something held him back. It was as if his father was a stranger.

Slowly his father raised his head and looked at him. Sean held his breath. Then his father reached out his hand. Sean reached forward with both hands and grasped it. His father's grip was firm.

'Sean,' his father said, his voice no longer firm and vibrant. 'I always knew you would come.'

Sean nodded, not trusting his own voice. 'How is Liam?' his father asked. 'And ... and Beatrice? And my father? Are they well?'

Sean nodded again and his father smiled for the first time. 'Are you OK, Dad?' Sean asked, finding his voice as hope surged through him.

'Oh, not so bad, I suppose. I missed you all. Sometime I thought I would never see you again. And I was so worried about Sergei. They told me he was dead, but I can't believe anything they say. Do you know if it's true?'

Sean nodded and quickly explained the recent events to his father.

'Poor Sergei,' Denis Gunne said. 'He was a good man. And a brave man. At least they can't hurt him anymore. And you did well,' he added, looking at Sean. 'I'm proud of you.'

'But I let myself be caught,' Sean said, angry and shamed by his failure. 'If I hadn't been so stupid ...' He stopped as the door was unlocked and a man brought in a tray. There were bowls of soup and bread rolls.

'That smells good,' Denis Gunne said when the man had left. He took a bowl of soup and a bread roll and smiled at Sean.

Sean smiled back, aware that they were both putting on an act for each other. Soon they would have to face the reality that they were prisoners, with little hope of escape.

His father, he knew, must be close to despair. The death of Bukanov had obviously affected him greatly, and no doubt he blamed himself for it. But neither despair, nor blame, would get them out of this place. For that they would need clear minds. But he would lead up gently to what had to be faced.

'Do you know what you're supposed to be doing here?' Sean asked.

'Only what I've been told,' his father said.

'About cloning?' Sean asked. 'And using stem cells?'

His father nodded. 'That's what they've told me,' he said. 'But I don't think it's the whole truth. I think there's something else Hawk wants.'

'But what?' Sean asked.

'Oh, he wants to perfect human cloning all right. I don't doubt that. But it's not simply to harvest stem cells. I think he wants to achieve more than merely to walk again.'

'But what more could he want?' Sean asked.

'Immortality,' his father said quietly. 'I know he wants to

clone himself to obtain stem cells to cure his paralysis. That destroys the embryo, of course. But I believe that he might also want to allow one of the cloned embryos to survive and develop into a human being. I think he wants to create a baby who will grow up, not to be his son or his brother, but a living breathing mirror image of Hawk himself.'

+   +   +

'I think I've worked out the clue,' Liam said to Jackie when she called later that afternoon. He was in his den, the table strewn with books and bits of paper. She glimpsed a section of the cover of one book and noticed that the word 'pattern' was prominent, superimposed on a ball of wool.

Despite the excitement in his voice, Liam looked grim. And though he smiled at her, the emotion didn't touch his eyes. She took the chair beside him.

'I failed miserably with the anagrams,' he said. 'Nothing I came up with made any sense. That was when I decided to try a different approach. I realised that Sean couldn't have had that much time to work on the clue. He phoned Granddad around nine last night and the email was sent from London this after-noon. He'd have had to get some sleep in between, so he'd hardly have had time to compose an elaborate anagram.'

'I decided then that the clue wasn't an anagram. It was some-thing else. And if he was sending a clue, wouldn't it be a clue to where he was being held prisoner?'

'And you've figured out where that is?' Jackie said, unable to keep the anxiety or the excitement out of her voice.

'I'm nearly sure,' Liam said. 'But I want to see what you think first. OK?'

'OK.' Jackie nodded.

'Right.' Liam frowned, as if gathering his thoughts. 'I decided that the clue had to be in the reference to knitting,' he began, 'because it doesn't make sense. You hadn't agreed to knit him a sweater and it's not his birthday. So what was he trying to tell us?'

'Now, he mentions liking the pattern, but doesn't name it. So I wondered if he couldn't name it because it would have given the game away. He put it in, aware that you would figure out it was a clue. But he couldn't let his captors know what he was up to. Does this make sense to you?'

'I think so,' Jackie said.

'Right,' Liam went on. 'So I looked up patterns in some old knitting books my gran gave Mom. Did you know, Jackie,' he asked, 'that there's a knitting pattern called Fair Isle?'

'Fair Isle,' Jackie echoed, staring at him. 'Fair Island. It has to be.' In her excitement she leaped to her feet and hugged Liam. His body was thin – it was like hugging a skeleton – but she could feel his heart beating strongly in his chest. He couldn't die, he wouldn't die: they were all mistaken.

Shaken by the thought, she released him and stepped back. She didn't want to face him immediately in case he saw the apprehension on her face. Instead she picked up the book that had caught her eye earlier, and opened it. 'Is this the one?' she asked, glancing at Liam, hoping that her fears were hidden by now.

'Yes.' He nodded. 'It's on page thirty-three.'

She flicked through the pages and found the relevant one. It showed a model wearing a round-necked jumper in beige wool with a distinctive pattern of horizontal rows of brown Xs and Os and inverted yellow Vs and Ws According to the caption, Fair Isle was a traditional pattern, originating in the Shetland Islands off the Scottish coast.

Jackie stared at the page. In her mind, there was no longer any doubt. Sean was being held on Fair Island and it was almost certain that his father was there too. She put the book down and turned to Liam, her face composed. 'What do we do now?' she asked. 'We can hardly take a knitting pattern as evidence to the gardaí. They'd only laugh at us.'

'And I know Mom won't believe it either,' Liam said. 'I've tried to explain all about Sergei Bukanov, but she doesn't want to know. She just wants Sean back.'

'She told me she's filed for divorce and is seeking custody of both Sean and myself. She thinks this is Dad's way of getting back at her and doesn't want to hear about anything else. She won't back us up if we go to the gardaí. Anyway, why would they believe such an unlikely story when they think they know the real one?'

'So it's up to us,' Jackie said.

'Up to you,' Liam said. 'I'm not going to be of much help.'

'You solved the clue,' Jackie said. 'I would never have figured it out.'

'You would,' Liam said.

'Maybe I could persuade my father to help,' Jackie said. 'He could go to Oldport and speak to some of his old colleague in the gardaí there. Or maybe he could get on to the island at night and take a look around.'

'That would be too dangerous,' Liam warned.

'I suppose,' Jackie said. 'But he *could* talk to his old colleagues. There would be no harm in that. And they just might take heed of what he has to say.'

'It might be our only chance,' Liam said. There was hope in his voice, but there was doubt there too. Jackie wanted to take away that doubt, and was determined to do everything in her power to do just that. If she succeeded, then Liam would be happy again. But if not ... she thrust the thought away, aware that it was something she didn't wish to contemplate or face.

TWENTY-THREE

Sean tried to come to terms with what his father implied, but found it impossible. He had believed Hawk when he spoke about cloning himself and using his stem cells to cure his paralysis. He had never contemplated the possibility that Hawk might want to clone himself, allow the embryo survive, develop into a baby and be born. Now he was forced to face the possibility that, according to his father, Hawk might want to do just that: to recreate himself and live forever!

But even if it were true, what could he and his father do about it? They were prisoners and his father would have to carry out Hawk's wishes or face the consequences. At best it would mean the black hole. At worst ... Sean didn't even want to think about that.

Taking a deep breath, he tried to convince his father of the gravity of their situation. 'If you refuse to co-operate,' he said, speaking earnestly, 'Costello will probably throw us both in the hole. You realise that, don't you, Dad?

Denis Gunne nodded and Sean pressed on. 'You have to co-operate, Dad,' he said. 'It's our only hope. And if you're successful in harvesting stem cells and curing Hawk's paralysis, then you might be able to cure Liam.'

His father stared at him, his eyes narrowed. 'But I don't agree with any of that sort of research,' he said. 'I thought you would have understood that, Sean. Even the harvesting of stem cells is morally and ethically wrong.'

'But what about Liam?' Sean protested. 'Surely he deserves a chance to live. You … you just can't stand by and watch him die. Not if there's something you can do to save his life.'

'But what about the consequences?' his father said quietly. 'Hawk wants to harvest stem cells from embryos. But an embryo is a potential human being. Can we destroy that potential life so that your brother can live? A death for a life? Is that what you want?'

It was a simple but powerful argument, and Sean had no answer to it. Could you justify taking the life of another human being so that someone you loved could live? But Hawk said that an embryo wasn't a human being. It was just a collection of cells with the potential for life. It was no more a human being than an acorn was an oak tree.

'What would Liam decide?' his father pressed on. 'If we gave him the choice, what would he answer?'

'I don't know,' Sean said. 'But should the choice be his alone to make?'

'Well, whose choice should it be? Yours? Mine? Hawk Silvermann's?'

'I don't know,' Sean said again. He shook his head, staring straight before him, not daring to look his father in the eye. The euphoria he'd felt earlier at the thought that Liam might have a chance to live was slowly ebbing away.

'As I've already said,' his father went on. 'I don't think that Hawk just wants to walk again. I think he has thought beyond that and wants to clone himself and go on cloning himself so he can live forever – have eternal life on earth. That's against the laws of nature and the laws of God.'

'And if there is no God?'

'There is still nature and its laws. Perhaps the world was created by chance as some scientists claim. But even so, it's still

147

governed by natural laws – by the cycle of birth and life and death. There's a line over which we must not step. What Hawk Silvermann proposes oversteps that line and that is dangerous.'

'But what about progress?' Sean insisted. 'Surely we can't stand in its way. If we do, aren't we being blind? What would have happened if all those who came up with new inventions had stopped experimenting because they thought that evil, and not good, would come of it?'

'Every new invention brings its own evils,' his father said. 'Look at nuclear energy. We first used it to make a bomb to kill people. And it has the potential of wiping out mankind and turning the world to desert. Yet many of those who worked on its development saw only the good that would come from it, not the evil.

'It's the same with cloning. Some good would come from it – perhaps Liam *could* be given the gift of life. But do we want men like Hawk Silvermann or Costello to live again? Do we want their evil perpetuated? Would we want the tyrants of history to live again: the Hitlers and Stalins? Or today's tyrants with so much blood on their hands?'

'But Hawk might not want any of that,' Sean said. 'You don't really know.'

'It's true that I don't know for certain what his plans are,' Denis Gunne agreed. 'But I have met his type before; once they see what is possible they always want to push the boundaries further and further. In any event, if we do perfect human cloning here, then inevitably the technique will be abused at some time, if not by Hawk Silvermann, then by someone else.'

'I don't want any part of that. I gave up research because I saw where it was leading. As a doctor, I want to help people – give them a better life. But not at any price. And from what I read recently, it seems probable that soon it will be possible to grow stem cells from ordinary blood cells. I would be more than willing to assist in that sort of research, especially if it gave Liam a better quality of life. Or if it could save his life. But what Hawk wants goes against my conscience.'

'So you're going to refuse to co-operate?' Sean said. 'Despite the consequences for both of us.'

'No, no,' Denis Gunne said. 'I am going to co-operate. I have no choice. It's not just myself I would be condemning to the black hole. I have to think of you now too. I will co-operate for the time being, but only so that I can have an opportunity to escape and tell the world about this place and bring these people to justice.'

'Hawk may have promised you our freedom when his project is complete and he may intend to keep his word. But I don't trust Costello. He's the one who holds power over life and death here. He's the one we must really fear.'

'And if we don't escape ... What then?'

'I don't know, Sean. I'll face that hurdle when I come to it. Meanwhile, we must ensure that we're free to move around and have the opportunity to plan and execute an escape. We must do nothing to jeopardise that.'

+   +   +

That evening, Jackie tried to persuade her father to see her point of view concerning Sean's disappearance and the clue in the email. But she was fighting a losing battle. 'Surely the logical explanation is that Sean has gone to his father as he says,' Stephen Howley pointed out.

'But what about that bit about the knitting?' Jackie persisted.

'Perhaps there's a simple explanation,' her father said. 'Sean may have included it in the wrong email? Maybe that message was intended for his girlfriend and he put it in yours by accident. Maybe he was in a hurry or was agitated. And he would certainly have been excited to be with his father again.'

'But he hasn't got a girlfriend,' Jackie said shortly.

'No?' Her father stared at her and made a face. 'How can you be so sure?'

'I just know,' she said. 'But let's forget that. Let's suppose it is a clue. Then it points to Fair Island. I think Sergei Bukanov swam from there. And if he mentioned Doctor Dolittle, then he must have been with Sean's father. And what about the break-in here and my rucksack being stolen? And now with Sean missing. .. it's obvious that something's going on.'

'But what about the men who called to Sean's grandfather's house last night?' her father countered. 'Why claim that Denis Gunne sent them?'

'To mislead us,' Jackie said. 'They used that story to hide the fact that they abducted Sean. The email's part of that ruse. And it's worked. Everyone believes he's gone with his father. Even you believe it. But that clue in the email, along with all those other things, proves it isn't so.'

'But why kidnap Sean?' Stephen Howley insisted.

'I don't know,' Jackie said. 'That's why I want you to go to Oldport this weekend and speak to your garda colleagues there and persuade them to investigate further. Maybe you could even sneak onto Fair Island and look around.'

'It's private property,' Stephen Howley said. 'I just can't sneak onto it. It's against the law. And anyway, security is very tight there.'

'But you could speak to your colleagues,' Jackie said. 'And if it means saving Sean and his father ...'

'He must mean a lot to you,' her father said.

'It's ... it's more for Liam than anyone else. And it's the right thing to do.'

'That I do agree with,' her father said. 'And, after all, you may be right.'

'You'll go then?' Jackie said.

'Maybe on Sunday. That's all I can promise. I'm going to Limerick tomorrow and hope to be finished there by evening. If I am finished, then I'll drive to Oldport tomorrow night or on Sunday. You can go down yourself by train and I'll meet you there.'

Thanks, Dad,' Jackie said, aware that this was as much as she could hope for. Her father quite obviously thought that the evidence she was putting forward was flimsy. But to her it was rock solid. Sean and his father were prisoners on Fair Island and she and Liam were the only ones who really believed it. If they didn't act, they might never see them again.

+   +   +

'You're seeing sense at last,' Costello said when he returned to Sean's cell to be told by Denis Gunne that he would co-operate. 'Now I'll give you the conditions. You'll work on the project under Brandt's supervision. Your son must live in the tower and you may meet once a day, in the evening. If either of you cause any trouble, there will be no more meetings and I'll have Sean thrown in the hole. Right?'

They had no choice but to agree and Costello granted Sean some more time with his father. They no longer discussed cloning or ethics, speaking instead of the events of the past week. Sean learned of the CD his father had given Bukanov and that Costello had retrieved it. It explained the burglary at Jackie's house and the theft of her rucksack. Sean also learned that the company in Texas that had tried to recruit his father had been called Mirror Image, the same company that had interviewed James Stewart, the missing Glasgow scientist whose name he and Jackie had found on the Internet that day in Oldport library.

Denis Gunne also spoke about Hawk's mysterious morning visits to the strongroom. He had no idea what was kept in there, but obviously it was of great value to Hawk.

Sean didn't mention sending a clue to their whereabouts in the email. He didn't want to raise his father's hopes, aware that the chances of Jackie or Liam deciphering the clue were probably remote.

They were brought supper and were reluctant to part later when Costello returned to take Sean up to the tower. 'See you tomorrow,' his father said, hugging Sean before Costello took him away.

As he passed the strongroom with its steel door, Sean again wondered what the room contained. It had to be gold bullion or something like that, some possession that was extremely valuable to Hawk.

On his way up to the tower, Sean tried to spot the code Costello used to operate the lift. But the latter took care to conceal it. Up in the tower, Sean was shown his room. It contained a bed, a wardrobe, a television and video and a small collection of books. 'You will not bother Mr Silvermann,' Costello said. 'If you do, or break any of the rules, there will be consequences for you and your father.'

Then Costello took him to Hawk's study and left them alone. Hawk sat behind his desk, a chessboard before him. He contemplated the board for some time before he looked up. 'Your father is behaving sensibly at last,' he said. 'Now we will make some progress. When my dream has been accomplished, then we can all go free. Yes?'

Sean could only nod. The man repelled him, and he could never forgive either him or Costello for what they had done to his father. But he realised that it would be a good idea not to antagonise Hawk.

'Good,' Hawk said with satisfaction. 'Now, do you play chess?'

Sean was surprised at the question and the change of mood. After all that had happened, this man wanted him to play chess with him? 'I'm not very good,' Sean said.

'Neither am I,' Hawk said. He set up the pieces and held up a knight for Sean's perusal. 'The pieces are carved from whalebone,' he went on. 'I was told that a sailor on one of the old whaling ships carved them. They're supposed to be over a hundred and fifty years old.'

The knight was dressed in armour and seated on a rearing horse with flaring nostrils. Looking at the piece, Sean could easily imagine that the horse had been in battle.

'The detail is extraordinary, isn't it?' Hawk said. 'Just think that if that sailor was given a second chance to live he might be a world famous sculptor. He might be as famous as Michelangelo himself.

'Have you ever thought, Sean, of the part chance plays in our lives? If I hadn't crashed that day in Texas or if your brother had been born healthy, where would we be right now? It's all down to chance, isn't it? But what if we could beat chance? What then?'

Hawk's eyes glazed over. They seemed to stare into the distance, seeing nothing. A muscle twitched in his left cheek. He took deep breaths and blinked a few times. 'Let's play,' he said eventually, placing the knight on the board.

Hawk had too much experience for Sean, who failed to win or draw a single game. Hawk made no comment on this. 'It's time for you to go to your room now,' Hawk said. 'We will play again tomorrow. Oh, by the way, did Costello tell you there will be a fire drill in the morning?' he added. 'My brother lost his life in a fire when we were children and I have a particular dread of fire ever since. I don't ever want to see another person burned to death. There is also something in the castle I value more than my own life. And fire is one of the things that could destroy it.'

'Do you keep it in the strongroom?' Sean asked.

Hawk stared at him, something like panic in his eyes. 'What do you know about the strongroom?' he asked.

'Nothing,' Sean mumbled. 'I don't know anything. Only it looks like a strongroom and I... I thought that maybe you kept your valuables there.' Fear loosened his tongue. He couldn't control it. 'Whatever it is you don't want to be burned – gold and jewels and that ..'

'Yes,' Hawk said now. 'That's what I keep there: a jewel of the rarest kind.' His eyes grew darker. 'One day I will show you this jewel,' he added. 'One day the whole world will see it, and people will marvel at it. It will be the most wondrous of all the wonders of the world.'

He was trembling. His eyes gleamed like chips of black quartz. Sean was certain they were filmed over with moisture. Hawk closed them and slowly the trembling stopped. When he opened them again, he appeared to be in control.

'When you hear the fire alarm tomorrow,' he continued, 'you must go to the gate at the foot of the stairs leading up to the roof. The gate will open automatically. Wait there. Do not go up on to the roof unless you are told to do so'

'If there should be a real fire, Quigly will take me to the roof and you will accompany us. But don't let that worry you. We won't have a fire here. I insist on the most stringent precautions. So you can sleep without worry.'

'But how do we get off the roof?' Sean asked.

'My helicopter will take us off,' Hawk replied. It's the only way off the roof unless you're willing to jump. And I don't advise that. It's two hundred feet straight down onto jagged rocks, and if they don't kill you, the sea will. Now, off you go.'

Sean went to his room and got ready for bed. But he couldn't sleep and lay awake in the dark, thinking of Jackie and Liam. Had they worked out the clue? Did they even realise that it was a clue? Surely they did, but even if they had managed to decipher it what could they do?

He tried to bolster his confidence with thoughts of escape but it was difficult. He and his father had spoken of escape as if it were an inevitable reality. But he knew that getting out of this fortress would be almost impossible. What if they never escaped?

The possibility struck Sean like a blow. If that happened, he would never see his family again. The reality lodged in his brain and it was still there like a burr when sleep claimed him, despair hovering above him like a dark ghost ready to swoop down and engulf him.

TWENTY-FOUR

Sean was summoned to Hawk's study the next morning to play chess. They were on their second game when the fire alarm shrilled. Hawk broke off to watch the monitors. As he did so, Sean heard a whirring sound from the cabinet where the TV and video were housed.

Was that the video recorder, he wondered? Was Hawk

automatically taping the feeds from the surveillance cameras, and if so why? Sean watched the monitors as the pictures changed every few seconds, showing different parts of the tower and the complex.

On one monitor he noted Costello at the strongroom door. Costello punched in the code on the keypad and the door slowly swung open. What appeared to be steam billowed out. Hawk became even more intent as he stared at the monitor. He leaned forward and operated a small joystick attached to the keyboard. The camera zoomed in on the strongroom door.

Just then Sean sensed a presence behind him. He turned to find Quigly standing at the back of his chair. The man's normally inscrutable face was angry. He grabbed Sean's shoulder and almost lifted him from the chair. With his other hand Quigly gestured towards the door. Sean understood. He was supposed to be at the bottom of the stairs.

Reluctantly he rose and left the study, and took up his position by the steel gate. He pushed the gate and it opened a fraction. It was unlocked. Freedom beckoned him, and for a moment he was tempted to flee. But he realised that it would be pointless if there was no means of getting off the roof.

Just now he didn't wish to antagonise Hawk and be confined in the black hole. So he resisted the impulse to go onto the roof and see for himself if Hawk had spoken the truth. A plan was forming in his mind and for that he needed his freedom. And he also wanted to see what Hawk had on the tape he'd made. He wanted to be certain that the same routine was followed for each drill.

Sean waited by the gate until the alarm ceased and Quigly came to collect him. When he returned, the monitors were showing their usual selection of pictures, and Hawk was contemplating the chessboard.

'I ... I wonder if I could borrow some of your tapes some-time?' Sean asked. 'I have a video, but no films.'

'I'll see that you're provided with what you want,' Hawk said. 'Make out a list of films or anything else you require, and give it to Quigly. He'll see it's attended to.'

'Thanks,' Sean said, hiding his disappointment. He'd hoped that Hawk might have agreed to his borrowing some of the tapes so that he could sneak out the surveillance video as well. But that door was now closed.

They continued the game, which Hawk won. As Sean set up the pieces again, Hawk shook his head. 'That's enough for now,' he said. 'It is time for me to go down ...' He was suddenly fidgety, and pressed a button on the arm of the chair.

Quigly came immediately and Sean deduced, from what his father had told him yesterday about Hawk's visits to the stron-groom, that that was where he was now going. Would he be left here alone? Sean wondered. Or would Quigly lock him in his room?

Sean began to slip out of the study, hoping that Hawk would forget about him. But Hawk's voice stilled him. 'Wait,' he ordered. Sean turned slowly to face him. 'You may borrow the videos for now,' Hawk said. 'They belonged to Abraham Make sure you take good care of them, rewind them and leave them back.'

'Thanks,' Sean said. He took two Marx Brothers' videos from the shelf and retreated to his room before Hawk had an oppor-tunity to change his mind. Here he put on one of the videos, but kept the volume low so that he could hear the lift. As it began its descent, he ran back to Hawk's study to watch the monitors.

He saw Hawk emerge from the lift. Quigly walked behind him. To Sean's surprise, both men were dressed as if for a skiing expedition. He shook his head, unable to make sense of it. Costello stood by the strongroom door. Sean operated the joystick to zoom in on the keypad, but Costello's hand obscured it. He could see only the tiny screen where seven asterisks appeared, corresponding to the letters and numbers of the code.

The door swung open. Steam, or perhaps dry ice, billowed out. Hawk guided the chair through the door, followed by Quigly. Then the door swung shut.

Hawk stayed in the room for just over nine minutes. All the time Sean kept the camera trained on the keypad's screen. Suddenly seven asterisks appeared and the door swung open. Hawk and Quigly emerged. Sean caught Hawk's face in close up. He seemed distraught.

Sean returned the joystick to its original position and ran back to his room. He heard Hawk and Quigly return, and held his breath. But no one came to question him about going into the study, or interfering with the camera. He had learned little. He still had no idea what the strongroom contained. Nor did he know what code was used to open the door.

+   +   +

That afternoon Sean went along to the study to return the video tapes. There was no sign of Hawk or Quigly. He borrowed two more Marx Brothers' films and slipped what he surmised was the surveillance tape beneath his T-shirt. Clutching the two films to his chest, he walked back to his room.

When he felt certain that Quigly wasn't going to come and see why he had gone into Hawk's study, he took the surveillance tape, inserted it in the machine, and pressed Play. It was blank. Then he put the machine into reverse search mode. The morning's fire drill, with himself appearing in some frames, flitted by in reverse. He rewound the tape and played it through. Its sole contents were recordings of various days' fire drills. Hawk must really be paranoid about fire, Sean thought, to video each drill to ensure that his orders were carried out to the letter.

He noticed that the procedure was always the same: Costello opened the strongroom door and then stood by, ready and waiting. For those few moments, the room could be accessed. Sean realised that if he could get into the strongroom during a drill, or an actual fire, he could discover what was kept there. And already he had an idea of how he could manage it. Ironically, it was Hawk's own men who had shown him how it might be possible.

It would need precise timing and some luck. But if he could find out whatever it was Hawk guarded so carefully, and gain possession of it, he would have something to bargain with. If it was a jewel, as Hawk claimed, and he could get onto the roof with it, he could threaten to throw it in the sea unless his demands were met.

That might be their only hope of getting out of here. Hawk had promised to help Liam and to let them go when the project was a success. But yesterday Denis Gunne had expressed the belief that Costello would never allow them go free and that he was the one who would ultimately decide whether they lived or died.

If his father was right, then escape was their only hope. His plan to attempt to find out what was kept in the strongroom might fail, but it was worth taking a chance. It might be worth a few days in the black hole just to know what lay behind that door. Knowledge was power, Sean knew, and knowledge might yet give them the chance to escape.

He returned the tape, along with the films, and then went

along to the kitchen to make himself a snack. Tea and toast, he decided, was the perfect snack for the occasion, and he set about preparing it, carefully timing what he was doing.

TWENTY-FIVE

That evening, just before the time arranged for visiting his father, Sean went into the kitchen to set his plan in motion. He'd experimented earlier when he'd made the toast and, though he knew the timing could not be absolutely precise, he still hoped it would be accurate enough for his purpose.

Quigly was punctual and stood by the lift at exactly the appointed time. Sean joined him and waited for him to punch in the code. Quigly, like Costello, was careful. All Sean saw was six asterisks appear on the small screen.

The door seemed to take longer than usual to open and then close when Sean entered the lift. Then the journey down – a matter of seconds – seemed an eternity.

Sean was tense, waiting for the alarms to sound, not sure what would happen to the lift if they went off while he was inside. Would it stop and go back up? Or would it descend where it had been programmed to go? If it didn't reach the dungeons, his plan would fail.

The lift stopped with a jerk and the door slid open. Costello stood waiting. He didn't speak, but turned to lead Sean to his father's room. Now! Sean urged. Now! But no alarm sounded. Desperate to delay a few moments, he dropped to his knees, fiddling with his laces. Costello turned back. 'Move,' he barked. 'I'm not your-'

His words were cut off as the fire alarm suddenly began to wail, the din almost deafening. The sound seemed to fill the empty hallway. Sean heard Costello swear. The man knocked him aside as he sprang for the strongroom door and punched in the code.

Sean watched the door swing open with a hiss of compressed air. Vapour billowed out and, with it, an icy chill. The strongroom was obviously a giant freezer or cold store. Sean saw Costello speaking into his walkie-talkie. 'The tower kitchen?' he shouted. 'I'm on my way.'

He finished speaking and turned to Sean, clearly agitated. 'Wait here,' he ordered. 'Don't move.' Then he sprang for the stairs leading up to the tower. He punched in the code for the gate and his pounding footsteps echoed above the strident sound of the alarms.

Sean felt elated, with no thought yet of the possible consequences of his actions. His plan had worked. That was all that mattered. The element of surprise and shock had done the trick as he'd hoped. It was one thing to follow instructions in a practice drill, quite another to do so in reality.

The billowing air from the strongroom puzzled him. He had thought that Hawk kept the jewel he'd spoken of, along with gold bullion, locked away in the room and that the vapour was part of some elaborate air conditioning system. But none of those needed to be kept frozen. So what did the room contain?

He knew he had only seconds in which to act. It would not take long for Costello to realise that the fire alarm had been set off deliberately, and work out who was responsible. Sean clambered to his feet and turned towards the strongroom.

At the door, the chill struck him like a physical blow. He wrapped his arms about his chest for warmth. The room was small – hardly more than three metres by three. The walls and ceiling were covered with what looked like a steel mesh. Pipes, encrusted with ice, divided the mesh into sections.

The room was empty except for a steel table which stood in the centre. On the table sat what appeared to be a glass box. It was about two metres long, and about half a metre wide and the same in depth. Ice-encrusted pipes came up from the floor to the bottom of the box. The glass was frosted over so that whatever the box contained was not visible.

Sean stepped forward, more puzzled now than ever. The glass lid was held closed by two steel, spring-loaded clips. The cold was intense and the steel clips burned his fingers when, one at a time, he flicked them open.

The sound seemed loud in the silence, which was broken only by the hum of a nearby motor and the more distant hum of the cooling fans. So intent had he been, that he hadn't realised that the fire alarm had become silent. An angry Costello would be on his way back down from the tower. He had to act quickly.

Sean tried to push the lid upwards. But it was frozen. He heard shouts outside and the hiss of compressed air behind him. He turned. The door was slowly closing. Terror surged through him. What should he do? Stay and discover whatever secret the box contained? But that meant being trapped in the room. Or rush for the door before it closed?

But this might be his only chance to discover Hawk's secret. He hesitated, and then it was too late. The door hissed shut. He was trapped. Shivering uncontrollably, he turned back to the box. He grasped the clips and thrust at the lid. With a sudden snap, the ice seal broke.

Sean slowly pushed the lid fully open. Then, his heart thumping, he looked into the box.

+   +   +

When Costello reached the tower kitchen he found smoke billowing from the toaster. Two slices of bread had been put in the toaster, the browning control turned fully on, and the release mechanism jammed with a wooden spoon. The bread had burned, creating the smoke which had set off the alarm.

Relieved, but enraged at Sean Gunne, whom he knew had to be responsible, Costello barked an order into his walkie-talkie. A moment later the alarm ceased its wailing. Costello left the kitchen to find Quigly emerging from Hawk's room. Costello held up his hands, palms out, signalling that all was well. "A false alarm,' he signed. 'Inform Hawk that I am checking the system and will report to him shortly.'

Costello took the stairs to the dungeons two at a time. When he reached the bottom there was no sign of Sean Gunne. Panic gripped Costello. What if Sean had got out of the complex? It was unlikely, but he had to have had some reason for setting off the alarm. Perhaps he had found a means of escape, just as Bukanov had done. Before that they had thought that escape was impossible.

Was Sean with his father? Costello ran to the door of Denis Gunne's cell and punched in the code to unlock it. When a fire alarm sounded, all the doors down here locked automatically. It was a precaution against a mass escape attempt.

The fact that the door was locked confirmed that Sean couldn't be in the cell. He couldn't have reached the cell and got in before the door was locked. So where was he?

Costello glanced into the cell as the door swung open. An anxious Denis Gunne stood in the centre of the floor. Being locked in during a fire could not be a pleasant experience. 'What's happening?' he demanded. 'Where's Sean? Is he all right?'

Costello ignored him and pulled the door shut. He swung about and noted the wisps of vapour outside the strongroom. Of course! That's where he had got to. It was why he had set off the alarms. The boy was more resourceful than Costello had given him credit for. Well, it was time to teach him a lesson.

Costello ascended to the tower to make his report. 'A fault with the smoke detector in the kitchen,' he lied, not wanting Hawk to know that a mere boy had fooled him. Gunne would not tell Hawk what he had done. Costello would see to that.

'I'll have it replaced immediately,' Costello continued. 'At least we now know that the system works in a real emergency.'

He was dismissed, but before he left the tower he re-checked the kitchen and the boy's room. He found no sign that Sean Gunne had planned further surprises. Costello made his way back down to the dungeons and checked his watch. By his estimation, Sean had now spent over five minutes in the strongroom. It should be sufficient time to give him an experience that he would not forget in a hurry.

+   +   +

Sean stared into the box, his eyes widening in horror. He looked from top to bottom and back again, noting the shoes and the white trousers, the striped sweater with the baseball catcher's gloves resting on the chest. And finally he looked at the face of a dead boy, a frozen lock of blonde hair lying across his forehead.

Even in the throes of horror, Sean knew that the frozen boy was Abraham Silvermann. His face was unblemished; but for the ice and the extreme pallor, he might be asleep and not dead. And as he stared at the dead boy, Sean knew that Hawk had lied to him. Curing his paralysis was just a cover for his real goal. Even if Denis Gunne was wrong and Hawk didn't intend to clone himself forever, what was certain was that Hawk intended to clone his dead son and make him live again.

This was madness. The tragedy of his son's death had sent Hawk Silvermann hurtling headlong into the abyss. Nothing he said could be taken at face value; he couldn't be trusted.

Their only hope was to escape. They had to get out of here if they wanted to live.

One day Hawk's experiment would bear fruit. Then Abraham Silvermann would live again and he and Hawk would play baseball as they once had done. And what if Hawk was really mad and, when faced with death, decided to clone himself as Denis Gunne suspected? He would never die. He and his son could continually clone themselves and live forever, evil perpetuating evil until perhaps the world itself should end.

And Sean and his father would die. Even if Hawk were to allow them their freedom, Costello would never let them live to give evidence in a court of law against him.

Staring into the box at a dead boy who one day would live again, Sean hardly noticed the cold creep into his bones. He was already chilled from the insides out by what he had just seen and was being forced to face – that one day the dead could rise again on earth.

It was obscene, almost like going into a graveyard and seeing the dead come out of their graves, their rotting clothes hanging from their decaying bodies. How could you accept it?

Shivering uncontrollably, teeth chattering, Sean turned away from the box. He considered his predicament. He was trapped, and if Costello didn't release him soon, he would die. He would be found here with the dead body of a boy whose peace in death he was now determined should never be disturbed.

TWENTY-SIX

There was a keypad located just inside the strongroom door, and, desperate to get out, Sean punched in numerous different combinations of seven letters and numbers to try and find the code that would open the door. But it remained steadfastly shut. Behind him, the box continually drew his eyes as if the dead boy was beckoning him. What if he suddenly sat up, or spoke to him?

Although he knew that his fear was irrational, Sean ran to the box and pulled down the lid. Fingers numbed and fumbling, he refastened the clips. As he did so, a new fear was congealing in the pit of his stomach: What if Costello left him in here to die?

Costello could pretend he didn't know he was in the strongroom until it was too late. He was just the sort of man to do it. To someone like Costello, life was cheap. If that happened, Sean realised, he would be found dead and frozen like Abraham Silvermann in his glass coffin. For that was what the box was — a coffin — and this room would be a tomb for both of them.

Sean took a deep breath; he was allowing his fear to get the better of him. Costello needed him. Without Sean, he couldn't force Denis Gunne to work on Hawk's project. So it was highly unlikely that Costello would throw away his trump card just for the sake of revenge.

Sean's fears eased a little. But nothing could ease the cold. It seemed that the marrow of his bones had solidified into ice. He renewed his assault on the keypad, but his fingers were becoming numb and he could no longer locate the small keys with accuracy. Driven by desperation and fear, he started to bang on the door with his fists. But the blows would not even register on the thick steel.

His lungs hurt and it was an effort to breathe. He had almost lost heart when he heard a disembodied voice. The voice echoed in the chilled, foggy air and he swung about in terror to stare at the coffin. He was certain the lid would burst open and the dead boy sit up and stare at him with sightless eyes. He whimpered, primed by the desperate urge to run. But there was nowhere to run – no escaping this tomb.

' …learned your lesson.' The words cut through his panic and he recognised Costello's voice. There must be a speaker fitted in the room. He stared about, seeking the source of the sound, but it didn't seem to have any place of origin.

'Do you understand me?'

Sean didn't answer, and the voice repeated the words, this time with much more venom. 'Answer me, or you can stay and freeze to death.'

'Yes,' Sean said aloud, his teeth chattering. 'Yes, I understand..'

Beside him the control pad bleeped – seven distinctive bleeps in all – and seven asterisks appeared on the screen. With a hiss of compressed air, the door swung open.

Costello stood in the corridor, his face twisted with rage. Sean stumbled out into the warmth, shoulders hunched, arms clenched tight across his chest. The blow was fast and vicious; it almost knocked him down. He tottered, his head ringing, and a moment later tasted blood.

The door hissed shut. Sean wiped his mouth and saw the red stain on the back of his hand, which was grey from the cold. 'You won't forget this day in a hurry,' Costello spat. 'That I can guarantee. Now get back upstairs.'

Despite his acute discomfort, Sean felt a surge of relief. Costello was not going to put him in the hole. Sean lurched towards the lift. Costello pushed violently past him to punch in the code to open the door.

'Go to your room,' Costello ordered when they reached the tower, emphasising the command by a push in the back that almost floored him.

Sean stumbled along the corridor to his room. He was surprised not to be brought before Hawk. Maybe Costello didn't want Hawk to know what had just happened? That that could be to his advantage, Sean realised. With a surge of hope, he gained the sanctuary of his room, and turned defiantly to face his foe.

Costello loomed in the doorway. 'I'll deal with you tomorrow,' he said. 'Don't think I'm finished with you.'

'I thought Hawk was the boss,' Sean said. 'Won't he decide my punishment?'

'I'll decide,' Costello said.

'You're not going to tell him, are you?' Sean said. 'Because he's not a man to tolerate fools. Isn't that so?'

'Shut up,' Costello hissed. 'Or I'll shut you up.'

'No you won't,' Sean said. 'If you lay a hand on me, or attempt to hurt me or my father in any way, I'll tell Hawk what's happened. So it's your decision. Will I tell him about his dead son Abraham that I saw in his glass coffin? Will I tell him that I know that he hopes to bring the boy back to life as if he were God? Will I tell him about the CD Bukanov had – the one you were so desperate to retrieve?'

This bit about the CD was a sudden inspired guess. But it made sense and, judging by Costello's reaction, Sean had struck gold. Costello flinched and took a step into the room, his hands clenching and unclenching. 'No,' Sean said, shaking his head, his courage renewed. 'Don't even think of laying a hand on me. If you do, I'll tell Hawk everything. Now take me down to meet my father.'

He thought he had gone too far in calling Costello's bluff. But the man just nodded, and beckoned him on. Sean walked past Costello, half expecting to be struck another vicious blow. But no blow fell.

As Costello emerged from the room, Quigly appeared in the corridor. Sean watched the two men converse in sign language, Costello was, no doubt, making up some excuse for their presence here. Quigly withdrew and Costello summoned the lift.

This time Sean saw eight asterisks appear on the screen. It puzzled him. When Quigly had operated the lift just fifteen minutes or so before, only six asterisks had appeared. Did the code change with time or did Costello and Quigly use different codes? Yet the code to the strongroom had seven asterisks. It didn't make sense.

He abandoned the puzzle and savoured his small success. He now had a hold on Costello, and with each compromise, the man would be letting go some of his power. It might buy his father and himself the opportunity they desperately needed.

His father was locked in his cell and Costello operated the keypad to open the door. Again he was careless and Sean was able to see the number of asterisks in the code. Eight once more. 'You've got one hour,' Costello said. 'No more.' He turned and strode away as the door swung shut.

'There seems to have been an emergency,' his father said when he had hugged Sean. 'Was there a fire, or was it just another drill? Do you know?'

Sean nodded and, gathering his breath, recounted the evening's events for his father. Afterwards neither of them spoke for a long time. 'It's even worse than I feared,' Denis Gunne said eventually. 'I never guessed how crazy Hawk really is. I thought that maybe he wanted to clone the living. I never realised that he might want to clone the dead.'

'You were right, Dad,' Sean said now. 'When you said that evil would come of such a thing.'

As he spoke, he was coming to accept that cloning was wrong. If his brother Liam were to die right now, and it was possible to clone him and genetically modify the faulty genes that had caused his condition, would it be right to do so? The answer was most definitely no. How, as the clone grew from a baby, could he accept that this mirror image was Liam, even if perfect in every way, when it couldn't be him?

Liam was Liam, the brother he loved, the brother who made him laugh with his imitation of Wodehouse characters. Would his clone be able to imitate Jeeves or Bertie Wooster when he was old enough to do so? Would his clone have Liam's love of gardening and his knowledge of the world of plants and seeds? Or the love that he had for his family and friends, and that he drew, in turn, from everyone he came in contact with?

How could it be? The clone could no more be Liam than an effigy could be him. There was more to being human than simply a physical body. There was the spirit – the soul – whatever one wished to call it. It was that that made one unique, that distinguished one identical twin from the other.

If Liam's illness could be cured through a process of cloning and taking stem cells from the embryo, that just might be acceptable. But to create an embryo that would grow into a baby and then into a replica of the person? That was impossible to contemplate or accept. And to propose cloning the dead! That could never be.

Abraham Silvermann was dead. That was the reality. He was dead and could not live again. It was the law of nature that all living creatures died. To go against that law – against the law of

God, if one wished to believe in such a being, – was wrong. In that his father was right.

Sean knew that now for certain. And he knew too that from this moment on he had to do everything in his power to escape from here and stop this madness. If not, the dead would surely walk again and the living, his father and himself, would surely die.

TWENTY-SEVEN

Jackie Howley got the train from Dublin on Sunday morning. Before she left the house, her father rang to tell her that he would not be able to come to Oldport until late that afternoon and they would have to return to Dublin that night. Disappointed, Jackie began to wonder if the journey would be wasted.

When she reached Oldport, she wandered down to the jetty. The day was hot and humid, the sky dark and low. The air seemed to crackle with static electricity and the sea was like a restless animal.

An electrical storm was brewing and she decided to head for her grandfather's before it struck. As she turned away, she glimpsed a boat loom out of the gloom. As it drew near, she recognised it as the boat from Fair Island. Quickly, she ducked behind a parked van to watch.

The boat tied up at the jetty and two men disembarked. She

thought she recognised one of them as the man she had seen at Oldport station the previous Sunday morning. They walked past her hiding place and on towards the town. When they disappeared from sight, Jackie made her way to the boat. She squatted down to look into the cabin; it seemed to be deserted. A thought crossed her mind and she wondered if she dared act on it. What if she stowed on board, crossed to the island, and took a look around?

If she could establish for certain that Sean and his father were being held on the island, then she could summon the gardaí on her mobile phone. Or she could contact her father who would probably be on his way to Oldport by then. One way or the other, she would have Sean and his father rescued.

But her plan was fraught with danger. What if she was found on board? Or was discovered on the island? Then she would end up a captive too. But she reassured herself with the thought that she had her mobile with her, and could call her father as soon as she got onto the island and tell him where she was. That way she would be protected. But she couldn't phone now and tell him because he would forbid her to go.

The wind was getting up, heralding the coming storm. The boat rocked on the swell, the wind whistling in the rigging. Soon the rain would come hammering down. She would have to make up her mind quickly.

The jetty was almost deserted, few people venturing out while the storm was imminent. But the storm could work to her advantage. While everyone took shelter, she would be able to move about the island without fear of observation or detection.

She took a last look about to ensure no one was watching before clambering on board. There was no hiding place on deck; she would have to go down into the cabin area. Cautiously she descended the few steps to the door, and opened it.

The living area was spacious, panelled in dark wood, with seating on two sides. It had numerous built in cupboards and two low tables. She quickly crossed the deeply carpeted floor and entered a short passageway. On her right there was a narrow galley, to the left a room which contained two bunk beds. Up ahead, on a raised platform, was the cockpit.

She had once gone fishing with her grandfather on a similar boat belonging to one of his friends. She knew that up by the cockpit there should be a hatch giving access to the engine compartment. That would be her best hiding place.

She spotted the hatch right away. It opened easily on sprung hinges and she stared into the space. It was dark and smelled of engine oil. She would be safe there; unless there was an emergency, no one would come down.

At the thought of being enclosed in the smelly darkness, she took a step backwards. Once down there, she would have no means of escape except back up through the hatch. And even that route would be cut off when the men came back on board.

Uncertain, she stood up and peered out of the window onto the jetty. The men were hurrying towards the boat. They would be on board in seconds. She had no choice now. Jackie dropped to her haunches and lowered herself down the hatch, stepping onto a steel ladder. She descended a few rungs and pulled the hatch closed behind her. She felt the boat rock as the two men came on board. She was trapped.

She clung to the ladder in total darkness, praying that she wouldn't be found. She imagined herself being taken prisoner; then a thought struck her – suppose they didn't want to be burdened with her? What if they took her way out to sea and threw her overboard?

Hardly daring to breathe, she listened to the thump of feet on the deck. Then she heard a loud click. It was the door to the cabin area opening. Common sense urged her to climb down and hide. But she couldn't move. Above her, footsteps approached. They walked directly over the hatch, causing her to gasp. She bit her lip and tightened her grip on the rungs.

With a sudden roar, the engines started up just below her. The ladder shuddered as if it were alive, and had she not been holding on so tightly, she would have fallen. The sound escalated as the throttle was opened, and she felt the movement of the boat as it eased out from the jetty. As the revs increased further, she searched her pockets with one hand and found a tissue and fashioned two earplugs from it. They helped somewhat as the boat surged forward, bucking like a fairground ride.

She could hear nothing above the noise and realised that no one could hear her either. Now was her chance to climb down into the engine compartment and hide. But the noise and the darkness deterred her. Gritting her teeth, she clung desperately to the ladder, beginning to realise that she had been foolish to undertake this dangerous escapade.

+   +   +

On Fair Island the storm loomed on the horizon.

Sean had been woken early that morning by a deafening clattering sound. He got out of bed and looked from his window to see the helicopter lift off. It swung over the tower roof, banking sharply like a great dark insect. Then it disappeared from sight and the sound gradually faded.

Last night, after returning from seeing his father, he couldn't sleep. He had spent an hour or more thinking about the door codes, writing down his thoughts on a piece of paper. He picked up the paper and began to look at the notes and doodles he had made.

Costello had used a seven digit code to open the strongroom

door. Then he had used an eight digit code to operate the lift, open the gate and open Denis Gunne's cell. Quigly, on the other hand, had used a six digit code to operate the lift and a seven digit code to open the strongroom door. Both had operated the lift within fifteen minutes of each other, yet used different codes. Sean wrote down the names and beside them the number of digits:

Quigly: Lift – 6 digits. Strongroom – 7 digits.

Costello: Lift – 8 digits. Strongroom – 7 digits. Gate – 8 digits. Cell – 8 digits.

No matter how hard he stared at the words and figures, they didn't make sense. Costello and Quigly used two different codes to operate the lift. Costello used the same code for all but the strongroom. Here, Quigly also used the same code. Why did they both use the same code for the strongroom, or as Sean had come to think of it, Abraham's tomb?

He re-wrote the list, putting Costello first and substituting the name 'Abraham' for the strongroom.

Costello: Lift – 8 digits. Abraham – 7 digits. Gate – 8 digits. Cell – 8 digits.

Quigly: Lift – 6 digits. Abraham – 7 ...

He stopped and stared at the piece of paper. His heart began to beat faster. The names! The codes were in the names. He wrote them down again.

Abraham: 7 letters. Costello: 8 letters. Quigly: 6 letters.

He had cracked it. The code was simple and foolproof and could not be forgotten. Now he understood why the keypad had letters as well as numbers.

Barely able to conceal his excitement, Sean dressed and made his way to the kitchen. He didn't want to arouse Quigly or Hawk's suspicions by not having breakfast. He helped himself to muesli but could hardly eat it. Quigly came in and prepared a tray for Hawk.

Sean returned to his room and switched on the television. There was an early news bulletin and he was anxious not to miss it in case there was any report referring to himself or his father. There was no mention of them, but one item grabbed his attention. He listened with growing disbelief as the newscaster reported that an American businessman had arrived in Ireland to buy Fair Island from the reclusive Texan billionaire, Mr Max Silvermann. A spokesman for Mr Silvermann denied the claim, and also the rumours that the recluse intended moving his research operation from Fair Island to another, as yet unknown, location.

Sean stared at the television, hardly able to believe what he had heard. Did this mean that Hawk was giving up his dream of cloning? If so, Sean wondered, what would happen to his father and himself? Hawk or Costello could never allow them go free in these circumstances.

No, Hawk would never abandon his dream. And if he intended moving the project to another location, he would need Denis Gunne. And Sean knew too much to be left behind. Once they were moved, no one would ever find them. And when Hawk had achieved his dream, he would have no more use for them. Hawk, or more likely Costello, would have them both murdered.

Sean had hoped for time so that he could devise a foolproof escape plan. But time was no longer on his side. If any opportunity arose he would have to grasp it. It might be the only one he would ever have.

He switched off the television, and sat in a stupor. He heard a noise outside and peered out. Hawk was at the lift, dressed in his Goretex suit. He was going down to the strongroom. Quigly was beside him, similarly attired.

Now, Sean thought. It had to be now! For perhaps five or ten minutes he would have access to Hawk's computer. If he was correct about the codes, and could alter them, he would gain the upper hand. He could isolate himself up here and, with Hawk and Quigly locked in the strongroom, blackmail Costello into contacting the gardaí. Or even do so himself once he had access to the computer.

The gate on the stairs would prove difficult to breach. Hawk had intended these gates to be all but impregnable, as Costello had pointed out. Now that could be used against him. The helicopter being missing was an added bonus; they couldn't attack him from the roof.

Sean waited for the lift door to close, then ran to Hawk's study. Glancing at the monitor, he saw Hawk and Quigly emerge from the lift. Costello was waiting for them. As Costello punched in the code for the strongroom door, Sean sat in the chair before the computer monitor and placed his hand on the mouse.

He knew that the step he proposed taking was irrevocable. This could not be concealed from Hawk. Once he had accessed the computer system, he couldn't erase the record of his activities.

He could only hope that the system wasn't alarmed when he tried to access it. But why should it be? There was no reason to fear anyone breaking into it illegally from the tower.

He moved the cursor to the icon labelled 'Security' and double clicked. A window opened, requesting a password for access. Sean berated himself for being stupid. Of course there would be a password for accessing the system. But what was it?

The cursor blinked in the box, awaiting the correct sequence of letters and numbers. Sean glanced at the monitor. The strongroom door was open and Hawk was going inside.

Sean reckoned that he had about five minutes grace, hardly enough time to do what he wanted, never mind break a password. And if someone noticed that he had accessed the system, all hell would break loose.

He leaned over the keyboard and typed in the word 'Hawk'. The system refused to accept it, flashing a warning that it was incorrect and access was denied. He tried 'Silvermann', and then Hawk Silvermann, but with no success. He tried all the names he knew: Costello and Abraham, Corridan and Quigly, but none were correct. He sneaked another glance at the monitor. The strongroom door was closed. Costello leaned nonchalantly against the wall.

Sean tried 'Fair Island' and 'Mirror Image' with the same negative results. How many more attempts would he have before the screen flashed a security warning and the system shut down?

Chance wasn't going to provide him with the password. Sean realised that now. The probability was that the password was one that only Hawk would know – perhaps a credit card pin number or a telephone number. If it were something like that, then Sean would never crack it. But surveys had shown that people usually choose a password that related to something significant in their lives so that it was easy to recall. You might forget a phone or pin number. But you hardly ever forgot a significant event, like a birthday.

The photograph of Abraham Silvermann caught Sean's eye. As it did, it struck him just then what that event might be. And not only was it relevant to Hawk, but relevant to what he was trying to achieve here on Fair Island. It was a date of great significance – the date of Abraham's death.

Trembling with expectation, Sean reached down and keyed in the date: 15-07-2001. Nothing. He tried it without the dashes.

No success. He tried it backwards, but the message remained the same: 'Access Denied'.

Sick with disappointment, he leaned back in the chair and released the mouse. He glanced up at the monitor. Costello still lounged against the wall. Sean leaned forward as if he could see through the screen to the hidden password. But the flashing 'Access Denied' mocked him.

There were letters on the desk and Sean picked one up and glanced at it. It was a business letter, detailing the transfer of shares from one company to another. He was about to put it back down when the date caught his eye: 6-23-2002.

Sean was puzzled at first. Then he understood. The date was written American style, the month first, then the day. Almost unable to bear the tension, he leaned over the keyboard again and typed in the date of Abraham's death as 7-15-2001. But access was still denied.

He tried without the dashes: 7152001. Immediately, the hard drive whirred. The password box on the screen disappeared to be replaced with a set of menus. One was labelled 'Codes'.

He was in.

TWENTY-EIGHT

Once Sean was in the system, the rest was relatively easy. A screen opened with plans showing different areas of the tower and complex. Sean accessed the lower ground plan and another screen opened. Here each separate door and gate on that level were displayed, with icons beside each one.

Sean placed the cursor on the strongroom icon, and clicked. A window appeared showing a row of seven asterisks denoting the password. Below it was an option marked 'Clear Password'. Sean clicked it and a new window opened, requesting the existing password.

He typed in 'Abraham' and clicked OK. Almost immediately he was requested for a replacement password. He had already considered what this should be: 'Wodehouse'. Liam would see the humour of this when he eventually heard the story.

Sean clicked OK and was requested to re-type the new password. This he did and clicked OK again. Within two seconds a message appeared to inform him that the new password was accepted. Now Hawk and Quigly were safely locked in the strongroom. Without the new password they couldn't get out from inside and Costello couldn't unlock the door from the outside.

Sean could have whooped with joy. But there was no time for celebration. He set about altering the other passwords. He accessed the gate at the bottom of the stairs first. Two rows of asterisks, one of six and one of eight, appeared in the password box. Sean sighed with relief; he had guessed correctly.

He followed the same procedure, typing in 'Quigly' and 'Costello' for the existing passwords. The system accepted them and requested a new password. He choose 'Success', and moments later it was accepted.

The lift had three passwords, one of which contained four letters. Sean typed 'Hawk' for this one and then followed the procedure to the end. When prompted for his own choice of password, Sean typed 'Genius', and smiled for the first time.

He altered the password to his father's room to 'Dolittle', and then accessed the plan for the upper tower. Here he clicked on the icon for the gate leading to the roof and cleared the three existing passwords. But just as he was about to type in a new password, the computer bleeped. Simultaneously, a siren began to wail throughout the complex. The keyboard locked. Someone had become aware that he was in the system and had raised the alarm.

Sean could have cried out with frustration. All he'd needed was another few seconds to fully secure the tower and then he would have accessed the email and attempted to send a message for help. He reached for the telephone on the desk. As he did so, the winking light on the console faded and died. Simultaneously, the lights and monitors went out in the room, and the computer screen went dead.

His power had been cut off.

+ + +

Corridan throttled back the engines of the cruiser as the boat approached the jetty on Fair Island. His phone rang. He unclipped it from his belt. 'Corridan,' he said.

'We've got a problem.' It was Costello, and there was panic in his voice. 'Where are you?'

'Just at the jetty,' Corridan said. 'What's wrong?'

'No time for explanations,' Costello said. 'Get back here right away. We've got a serious emergency.' The connection was cut.

Corridan swore and cut the engines as the boat bumped gently against the tyre buffers. Granger was already on deck. He jumped onto the jetty and began to moor the boat. Corridan ran for the deck.

He was on the jetty when he remembered the coded card for

starting the engine. He had left it in its slot, but he didn't dare delay to go back for it. From the tone of Costello's voice, he realised that there was a very real emergency. Shouting at Granger to come on, Corridan leaped into the jeep that had brought them both from the castle that morning.

As Granger clambered aboard, Corridan started the engine. He floored the throttle and the jeep shot off towards the track to the castle, tyres spewing gravel under maximum acceleration.

+   +   +

When the engine revs were cut, Jackie knew that the boat must be approaching the jetty on Fair Island. Soon she felt the craft bump against the buffers and then the engines were switched off. The boat swayed wildly and she felt the thud of running footsteps overhead.

She removed the earplugs; her ears rang a little from the noise. She could hear the ticking of the engine as it cooled and the slap of water against the boat's hull. She listened carefully and heard doors slam outside and then an engine rev wildly. But there was no sound to indicate that there was anyone else on board. Nevertheless, she waited a few minutes before making a move.

She thrust open the hatch and listened. But there was no sound, other than the singing of the wind. She scrambled out and stared through the rain splattered windows. The sea was dark and heaving, heavy clouds seeming to hover just over the surface. Through the bow windows she could see the jetty and the research complex beyond. All seemed quiet and deserted.

She made her way up on deck. Rain was falling like vertical rods of solid water, and in the distance she heard the first rumbles of thunder over towards Oldport.

Satisfied that she was not being observed, she jumped onto

the jetty and ran to seek shelter in the lee of a boat shed. She wore only jeans and a sweatshirt, and by the time she reached shelter she was almost soaked through. She shook the rain from her hair, pulled the wet strands back into a ponytail, fastening it with a scrunchie from around her wrist. She gathered her breath and stood for some moments to calm her thumping heart. Then she reached in her pocket for her mobile phone.

+ + +

In Hawk's study, Sean sat in the chair, staring at the dead monitor screen. Costello had won. It was all over and the taste of defeat was sour on his tongue.

From what seemed faraway, he heard his name being called. It was Costello. Sean rose and walked out into the corridor. 'You!' Costello shouted, his voice booming in the stairwell. 'Get down here now.'

Sean crept to the top of the stairs. 'Yes,' he shouted back. 'What do you want?'

'The codes,' Costello ordered. 'Give me the new codes. If you do, I'll take no further action against you. But if you don't ...' He let the threat hang.

All was not yet lost, Sean realised. There was a still a chance for success. The doors and gate were locked and obviously couldn't be opened without the new codes. He still had a bargaining tool – time. Costello would eventually crack the codes, but that would take time. And time was something he didn't have. Hawk and Quigly could not survive for too long in the strongroom. Surely Costello would never crack the codes in that time.

'I have terms for you,' Sean called down.

'No terms,' Costello said. 'Give me the codes first. Then we talk.'

'No,' Sean said. 'Reconnect the power and give me access to email or the telephone. When I've contacted the police, I'll open the door to the strongroom. When they get here, I'll open the gate. They're my terms.'

'You're in no position to make terms,' Costello shouted. 'You've neither power nor access to email or telephone. So there's nothing you can do. Now I'll count to three and if you haven't given me the codes by then, I'll have your father brought out here. You want to hear him scream for mercy?'

'One ... two ... three ...' Costello's voice died away. Now Sean heard other voices from below. A moment passed, then another. 'Gunne! This is your last chance.' It was Costello again. 'Give me the codes or you and your father won't live to see another day.'

Sean shivered, but he didn't answer. Costello had discovered that he couldn't reach Denis Gunne. Now it was stalemate. Costello wouldn't reconnect the power or give him access to email or the telephone, and Sean wouldn't divulge the codes. There was no way Costello could guess the new passwords Sean had created and there simply wasn't enough time for him to break down the gate.

Sean found himself faced with a dilemma. Could he allow Hawk and Quigly to die? Could he sit here, watching the minutes pass, knowing that both of them were slowly freezing to death in that room with the body of Abraham? The suits they wore would offer them a certain amount of protection. But how much? Could they survive for an hour? Or two or three? What was certain was that they could not survive indefinitely.

How long could he wait before he gave the code for the strongroom door to Costello? Once he'd done that, it was only a matter of time before Costello broke down the gate or cut through the door to his father's room.

Sean reached out and pushed the steel gate leading up to the roof. To his horror, it opened. He must have unlocked it when he cleared the passwords. What if Costello became aware of this? If the helicopter returned or someone scaled the tower ...

'Gunne,' Costello called again. Sean didn't respond. Instead he went back into the darkened study where the dead telephone and computer on the desk mocked him. He just didn't know how long he could hold out. But he was aware that each minute would seem like an eternity.

Somewhere towards the mainland, he heard a rumble. It was thunder. He walked to the window and pulled across the blind. Outside the day was dark as night. Cloud hung low in the sky and the sea was a black sheet rippling in the wind. As he watched, he saw lightning split the sky, and the rumble of thunder came again.

He dropped the blind and returned to the desk to stare at the dead computer screen. He had almost succeeded. Maybe he should have made the phone call before he reset the codes. But if he had done that, he might not have had time to lock the doors. If only ... 'Stop!' he told himself. What was the point of 'if only' now? It would just be a matter of time before Costello had both himself and his father in his power. When that time came, Costello would almost certainly kill them.

Sean shivered. Perhaps in his effort to save himself and his father, he had sentenced them both to die. They would never see Liam or his mother again. Everyone, including Jackie, would think he had lied and had simply disappeared with his father to escape the law. Sean slumped into the chair while outside the thunder rumbled.

+   +   +

On the mainland the storm raged. Rain fell as if the walls of some great reservoir in the sky had been breached. High in the clouds static electricity charges built up to millions of volts. The air in the vicinity crackled as if alive.

There was a loud crack and a jagged flash as a cloud discharged its enormous electrical potential and a bolt of lightning shot to earth. It struck the electricity sub-station on the outskirts of Oldport. The explosion was heard in the town and the blue flash was seen a kilometre away.

Transformers flared into twisted masses of charred melted metal. The acrid smell of burning filled the air. In Oldport and the surrounding area, lights flickered and went out. Machinery ground to a halt. Computer systems went dead. The mobile communication mast on the hill above the town lost all power.

The underwater cable carrying power to Fair Island shorted, cutting out the supply. The emergency generator came on. But as it was only capable of supplying a fraction of the power required on the island, most of the electrical systems shut down. The security system at the tower was one of the items not affected. It still functioned and the doors and gates remained locked. Radio communication with the outside world was not affected, nor was the internal telephone system.

In the grounds of the complex a second back-up generator for the strongroom immediately came to life. It had its own diesel supply and could operate for a week before it cut out permanently. The pumps in the cooling system continued to run.

By now Hawk Silvermann and Quigly were shivering from the intense cold. Quigly stood beside his boss where he sat in his powered chair. Time was running out for both of them. If the door wasn't opened within the next two hours then two more bodies would be found here, as cold and as stiff as the body of Abraham Silvermann in his glass coffin.

TWENTY-NINE

Jackie stared in disbelief at the display on her phone: No Network. With fumbling fingers she speed-dialled her father's number. But the screen instantly displayed the same message: No Network.

The realisation that she was trapped on the island, and at the mercy of whoever might find her, was slowly sinking in. If these were the people who held Denis and Sean Gunne prisoner, and had driven Sergei Bukanov to his death, they would deal with her ruthlessly. She had no way of contacting the outside world or returning to the mainland.

The rain beat down relentlessly. Visibility was poor, which could work in her favour; it was unlikely that a sharp lookout would be kept in this weather.

She looked at the cruiser tied up at the jetty. It offered a means of escape. If she 'borrowed' it, she could make it safely back to the mainland. But then she would lose what might be the best opportunity she would have to take a look around. And she would also get into serious trouble for taking the boat.

She hesitated just for a moment. Coming to a decision, she slipped the phone into her pocket, abandoned her shelter and began to run along the track leading to the tower complex. The driving rain, coupled with the haze, hid the buildings as if behind a lace curtain. But if she couldn't see clearly, then anyone on lookout would have difficulty seeing her.

The storm was coming closer. Each time the thunder rumbled, her instinct was to clap her hands over her ears. A bolt of lightning hit the ground ahead of her and it took all her courage to go on. But she was determined to find out what she could while she had the chance.

Sean's freedom and that of his father – perhaps their very lives – might now depend on her alone. With this thought to encourage her, she ran on.

+   +   +

Corridan braked the jeep to a halt in the castle courtyard and leaped down from the driver's seat. Everything appeared normal except for the absence of the Rottweilers. 'Where are the dogs? he demanded of one of the guards as he entered the tower.

'Boss ordered them to be tied up,' the guard said. 'Some bigshot's due to visit this morning. He didn't want to scare him.'

Corridan nodded and hurried on down to the dungeon. Here an enraged Costello quickly outlined the situation. 'This looks like the end,' Corridan said. 'Maybe we should get out while we have the chance.'

'If only the chopper was here,' Costello said bitterly. 'But it won't return until the storm is over. The pilot contacted me on the radio to say he was going to wait at the airport until the storm blew out.'

'Can't you order him to fly?' Corridan said.

'I tried persuading him,' Costello said. 'But he refused. His passenger won't fly either. Apparently the Learjet was landing just as the storm broke and the man was terrified out of his wits.' Costello looked at his watch. Ten minutes had elapsed since Hawk and Quigly had been locked in the cold room. Time was not on their side.

'Should you switch off the cooling system?' Corridan said.

Costello shook his head. 'Hawk absolutely forbids it. Anyway, it would have no immediate effect. It would be hours from now before there was any significant drop in temperature.

By then Hawk would be long since dead.'

'So it looks like it's all over,' Corridan said.

'Not yet,' Costello said. 'Gunne can't make contact with anyone, so we don't have to worry about him. Our main problem is releasing Hawk and Quigly before it's too late. When we've done that, we can deal with Gunne. Right now, Dubrek is trying to break the codes. Gunne hadn't got round to altering the codes on the doors to the other scientists' rooms and I was able to release Dubrek. But he's not optimistic he can break the codes in time. So meanwhile, I want you to bring up cutting equipment and cut through the strongroom door.'

'That's specially treated steel,' Corridan said. 'It would take hours to cut through it.'

'Then, we'll cut through the gate to the tower instead,' Costello shouted. 'Once I've got my hands on Gunne, I'll have the new codes in seconds.'

Corridan nodded. 'I'll go get the cutting gear,' he said. 'I'll be through the gate in no time at all.'

'Right,' Costello said. 'I'll radio the chopper pilot again and tell him to fly back here as soon as it's safe. He can explain to the client that the island has no power right now and arrange for him to go to a local hotel. When power is restored, we'll have him picked up. If Hawk isn't released by then, it'll be too late, and we'll make a run for it. I'll speak to the pilot of the Learjet too and tell him to be ready to fly us out at a moment's notice.'

Corridan stared at Costello, but didn't speak. Then turning, he dashed back up the stairs to the ground floor. He raced out into the rain to the jeep and headed back to the jetty and the store where the cutting equipment was kept.

+   +   +

With the heavy rain and the rumbling thunder, Jackie almost didn't hear the sound of the engine as the jeep raced towards her. It was only at the last moment she saw the glare of headlights through the rain and haze. She leaped off the track and lay prone on the wet heather, aware that she was visible to anyone in the vehicle who cared to look.

The jeep came roaring out of the gloom like some gigantic monster, its eyes blazing. Jackie pressed her face into the heather and clenched her own eyes tight shut. She felt the vibration of the vehicle as it approached.

She tensed, waiting for it to screech to a halt, prepared to leap to her feet and run. A spray of gravel struck her and she almost cried out with relief. The jeep hadn't stopped. She scrambled to her feet and stared after it. Its rear lights painted the haze with streaks of red, like blood, and again she shivered.

Gathering herself, she pressed on, but she was more wary now. The tower loomed out of the haze, its bulk dark and menacing and sinister. To her surprise, the gates stood open. She stopped and, as this fact sunk in, terror seized her. She remembered the dogs they had seen patrolling the perimeter when they were on her grandfather's boat. If they sensed her presence, they would surely charge out and attack her. Would they have savaged her to death before anyone could come to her rescue?

She held her breath. No dog barked. She peered into the haze, but no dogs or guards were visible. But she couldn't muster the courage to enter.

Instead she stepped off the track onto the heather, moving along by the chain link fence. It had been erected quite close to the walls of the complex, the narrow space within gravelled over. She reached the spot where the walls joined the tower itself and stared upwards.

Despite the low cloud and haze, she could clearly see the battlements. She'd been so focused that she hadn't noticed that the rain had eased and visibility was improving. As a flash of lightning illuminated the scene, it was easy to imagine soldiers in armour crouched up there, arrows at the ready.

What now, she wondered? She hadn't thought this through at all. She should have waited for her father, but it was too late now.

She took out her phone and stared at the display, hoping against hope that she would have a connection. But the display still read 'No Network'. She was on her own. There was no hope of anyone coming to her aid, and no one knew she was here.

She heard the sound of an engine and turned to see headlights cutting through the haze. The jeep came racing back along the track and entered the complex As it did so, the gates swung shut behind it. Now she couldn't even get inside.

+   +   +

Up in the tower, Sean had grown restless. What was happening? He prowled the rooms like an animal scenting danger. His watch told him that time rapidly was slipping away. Every passing second brought the threat of death to Hawk and Quigly still closer.

Nearly twenty minutes had elapsed since they had been locked in the strongroom. How long could they survive? He'd thought perhaps an hour at least, but maybe it was much more. What if he was wrong? Could he just wait here knowing that two men might be dying below him and that at a word from him, they could be saved? How soon would it be before Costello acted? So far he seemed to have done nothing. Sean knew that he must be desperately trying to crack the new codes.

He heard a commotion below and crept to the top of the

stairs. Metal clanked against metal. Moments later there was a hissing sound and then a whoosh and a roar like wind blowing through a narrow gap.

An intense blue light flickered in the stairwell, illuminating the stone walls so that they seemed to shimmer and tremble. A moment later came the stench of burning – an acrid metallic smell. Costello, Sean realised, had got oxyacetylene cutting equipment and had begun cutting through the gate at the foot of the stairs.

How long would it take to cut through? Five minutes? Ten minutes? However long, the end would be the same. Costello would take him, and he would be forced to reveal the new codes. Then he and his father would surely die.

His only hope now was to get out of here. Could he manage somehow to climb down from the tower and get out of the complex? It was a slim possibility but, determined to act, he climbed to the roof to investigate.

The flat roof was square, edged with battlements on all four sides. The aerials and dishes for the communication facilities were located on the side that overlooked the sea. The leads snaked across the roof, disappearing into junction boxes fixed to the roof itself. Seeing them put an idea into Sean's head. He could use the cables as a rope to climb down from the tower.

He hurried across and looked down to the courtyard. The only exit was through the archway. Beyond that, the newer buildings stretched away on either side to the gates. The other two landward sides of the tower looked down onto narrow gravelled areas between the tower walls and the chain link fence. The only possible escape route, if he climbed down here, was over the top of the fence.

He checked the seaward side. Waves crashed against the foot of the cliff sixty metres below. It would take nerves of steel to climb down here, and even if he succeeded, what then?

As he stared down at the thrashing waters below, Sean knew that he would not survive long in that maelstrom. He would drown, or be dashed to death on the rocks. And even if he managed to reach the open sea, what then? He could never reach the mainland from here and even if he tried to, Costello would soon have him picked up.

He turned away, taking deep breaths to ease the queasy feeling in his stomach. It seemed hopeless to attempt to climb down from the tower. But he knew he couldn't just wait around doing nothing. He turned away and, glancing through a gap in the battlements on his right, caught a movement beyond the fence. There was someone out there. Instinctively he ducked low and peered out. A gasp escaped his lips. Even from up here, and despite the haze and the rain, he recognised her. It was Jackie.

A confusion of thoughts bombarded his mind like snooker balls shooting out after a break. Was he hallucinating? How could Jackie be out there? How did she get here? What was she doing? What would happen if someone else spotted her?

The last thought spurred him to action and he straightened up. He must warn her. It was because of him she was here.

She was moving towards the fence. Sean cupped his hands to his mouth and called her name. But the sound was lost in a rumble of thunder. He waited for a lull, but before it came, she had turned away from the fence and made to move off. Sean felt the weight of despair settle on his shoulders.

And then, as if some sixth sense warned her, Jackie turned and stared up at the battlements. She took a step backwards, clamped one hand over her mouth as if stop herself from shouting, and waved frantically with her other hand. He waved back.

He watched her stare at the fence. Then she reached out with both hands and grasped it. She clearly intended climbing it, despite the rows of razor wire on top.

She glanced up. He shook his head frantically and gestured with his hands that she should not climb up. Now that he had her attention, he made hand over hand gestures to indicate that he intended climbing down. She looked alarmed, her eyes scanning the vertiginous drop from the battlements.

He raised his hands in a questioning gesture. What choice did he have? She pointed towards the jetty, then cupped her hands, forming a receptacle, before pointing towards the sea. Then she pointed back up at Sean and made hand over hand gestures as he had done.

She wanted him to climb down on the seaward side! But it didn't make sense. He shook his head.

Again Jackie pointed towards the jetty and cupped her hands. Then she swung her cupped hands to draw a line from the jetty to the foot of the cliff.

Now he understood. Her cupped hands formed the shape of a boat. She was indicating that she would bring a boat to the foot of the cliff and that he should climb down to meet her. She must have crossed to the island on her grandfather's boat. Or procured a boat of some sort. But how come she hadn't been spotted?

Sean's spirits lifted. Giving Jackie the thumbs up sign, he watched her wave in acknowledgement. Then she turned and started to run back towards the jetty. He watched her until she disappeared from view, swallowed up by the haze. Only then did he make his way back down the stairs.

Acrid-smelling smoke was billowing up the stairwell. Below, at the foot of the stairs, the acetylene torch hissed and flared. The blue light, viewed through the smoke, was like a scene from some filmmaker's special effect's scenario. Were they close to breaking through? Sean wondered.

He needed something sharp to cut through the communication cables. Looking around, he saw a fire axe hanging beside the extinguisher and fire bucket. He grabbed the heavy axe and raced back up onto the roof.

Picking out the longest lengths of cable, he hacked through them, hoping the wooden handle of the axe would insulate him from any electrical shock if they were carrying current. When he had what he judged to be sufficient cable to reach the sea, he knotted them together with difficulty, acutely aware that his life would soon depend on them.

+ + +

Down in the dungeon, Corridan was operating the cutting torch, his helmeted head illuminated by the blue flame, sparks flaring and smoke billowing about him. His prediction that he would be through the gate 'in no time at all' had been overly optimistic. The cutting process was slow, the metal glowing white hot and sizzling where the flame struck it.

Costello watched impatiently, his anxiety growing stronger by the minute. He had begun to think more and more of saving his own skin. Hawk and Quigly were surely doomed. They would never cut through the gate in time.

If Hawk died, Costello was determined to make his getaway as soon as the chopper arrived. When he'd last spoken to the pilot, the man had assured him that the storm was easing and that he should be airborne in the next half hour.

Costello looked at his watch. The chopper should be on its way right now. If he hadn't got to Sean Gunne by the time it arrived, and if there was no response from Hawk by then, Costello intended to flee. He wasn't short of funds; Hawk paid well for his services and there was nowhere on Fair Island to spend the money. When he got out of this God-forsaken place, Costello intended having a good time with the money he'd earned. Then he would find himself a new employer. There was no shortage of those willing to pay good money for someone with Costello's 'special talents'.

THIRTY

Sean secured one end of the knotted cable to the stanchion of a communication dish. Then, taking the other end, he dropped it over the battlements, where it snaked down the tower wall and cliff face to the sea below. It was a sixty metre sheer fall, but to Sean it looked like a drop into an abyss. And if he did manage to make the treacherous descent, there was still the angry sea to face. How could Jackie manoeuvre a boat through these rocks?

He realised that he had made a terrible mistake. He should have insisted that, instead of coming to rescue him, she head for the mainland and raise the alarm. That would have been the sensible thing to do.

Had they nearly cut through the gate, he wondered? Any second now they might come pounding up the stairs and all would be lost. The possibility urged him to action and he scrambled onto the battlements. The sea below him was grey in the dim light. He could hear the angry slaps of the waves against the rocks. Their jagged peaks were like the teeth of some ferocious animal, eagerly awaiting his fall. But to remain here meant certain death too. And not just for himself, but for his father and also for Hawk and Quigly. They would not survive much longer in the strongroom. It was imperative that he reach the mainland and summon help.

He grasped the cable. Its plastic coating was smooth and slippery from the rain. If he lost his grip, he would slide down helplessly, burning the palms of his hand through to the bone.

Gritting his teeth, he swung his legs over the edge. He wrapped the cable about his right calf to take some of the strain. Then, grasping the cable tightly in both hands, he eased fully over until he was hanging in mid air.

His mouth was dry. His arms and leg trembled under the pressure exerted on his muscles. Fear gripped him. But this was no time for fear. Not daring to look down, he began his descent.

+ + +

Jackie raced back to the jetty, ignoring the stitch in her side. Her mind was in turmoil. Sean's life and that of his father depended on her now.

The rain had eased and the thunder was moving away northwards. A welcome breeze freshened the humid air. She stealthily made her way to the jetty and onto the boat, not certain if anyone was on board. But she didn't have time to check. Going straight to the cockpit, she pressed the starter. To her utter relief, the engines fired first time. She felt their vibration beneath her feet and it gave her courage.

She ran on deck to cast off and only then saw the man at the gate to the research buildings beside the jetty. The engines must have alerted him.

'Hey, you,' he shouted, waving his hands.

His words galvanised her into action. She ran to the mooring hitch and began to untie the thick rope. It was wet and the knot was tight. As she worked frantically with fingers that seemed to have become thumbs, she saw him begin to move towards her.

As the knot came loose, she heard his pounding footsteps. It gave impetus to her legs. She ran for the cabin and raced through to the cockpit. As she leaped for the wheel, she yanked the throttle fully open. The boat reared like a bucking horse. Jackie clung to the wheel as the craft threatened to throw her backwards. Then it surged forward, its bow pointing towards the sky.

They were rushing towards the other side of the horseshoe shaped jetty. Collision seemed inevitable. Desperately, Jackie spun the wheel to the left and closed the throttle. The bow dropped and the boat swung about. She clung tight to the wheel as the boat slid along the rubber buffers and then cleared them. Ahead was the open sea. Sobbing with fear and relief, Jackie opened the throttle again. The engine revs increased and the bow rose as the twin propellers thrust the boat through the water, spray flying by on both sides.

Jackie risked a backwards glance. The man stood on the jetty, staring after her. He shook his fist, then turned and ran back towards the complex. She knew he would raise the alarm, but there was nothing she could do about that. She could only hope now that luck might be on her side.

She turned back to the wheel and swung it about, setting a course for the cliff. Her priority now was to reach Sean and rescue him. As the boat sped through the water, she reached for the radio mike and clicked it to transmit.

+   +   +

The internal phone rang at the control centre in the castle. Moments later a frightened security guard pounded down the stairs to the dungeons. 'A call from the jetty,' the man panted to Costello. 'There's an emergency. Some girl's stolen the boat.'

Costello swore. Was there nothing that couldn't go wrong today? He grabbed the nearest phone. 'This had better not be true,' he raged into the mouthpiece.

'It is. It is.' The voice on the other end of the line betrayed the man's fear. 'There was a girl at the jetty. I tried to stop her but she stole the boat and got away.'

Costello swore again. How could a girl get onto the jetty and steal the boat? And no one should be able to start the boat. Bloody Corridan! He must have left the card in the ignition.

It had to be the Howley girl, and now she had got away. If she reached the mainland and raised the alarm ... She had to be stopped at any cost.

'I'll send the speedboat from here right away,' Costello said. 'We may just have enough time to catch up with her before she reaches the mainland.' He hung up and began to bark orders. Then he ran up to the control centre.

He desperately needed the chopper. If it was close it could stop the girl or at least hinder her progress until the speedboat caught up with her. He grabbed the radio mike and called up the pilot. There was only the noise of static in his ears. His only link with the helicopter was cut off. He hesitated, then ran back down to the dungeon. Corridan had nearly cut through the gate. Within minutes they would have Sean Gunne. Costello reckoned it would take no more than thirty seconds to extract the new codes. There were, after all, means of gaining information if one was ruthless or desperate enough. Hawk's life could yet be saved. And if the speedboat could catch up with the girl, it might still be possible to salvage the situation.

The strain on Sean's arms and leg was beginning to tell and his palms were sore where the cable burned into the flesh. But he had to push on. There was no way back from here.

The rain had ceased and the thunder had moved away. He welcomed the fresh breeze that ruffled his hair and cooled the sweat on his face. Hand over hand, he dropped lower and lower.

He was over halfway down when he heard the note of an engine. Risking a glance over his shoulder, he saw a boat heading towards him. It had to be Jackie.

New-found hope gave him a fresh burst of energy, and the strain, or pain, didn't seem so bad now. The engine noise rose and fell as Jackie circled the area, waiting for him to reach the water. From there he would have to swim for it. The boat could not come any closer because of the rocks.

He thrust that problem from his mind and concentrated on the descent. When he heard the shout, it startled him. He looked up to see faces peering over the edge of the battlements. Costello was on the roof; the gate had obviously been breached.

He glanced down. The water was about four metres below him, seething amongst the rocks. He was almost there. He continued his descent, eyes fixed on the cliff face again. He had gained a metre before the cable jerked in his hands. Then he felt himself being hauled upwards.

Below him, the boat sounded a warning. But he didn't need any warning. He realised his situation was perilous. He glanced down again. The end of the cable was just clearing the water. He could still make it if he acted now. The time for caution was past. He released his leg from the cable, taking his whole weight on his arms. It was agony to hang there in mid air, but if he fell, even this distance, he could still kill himself.

He gripped the cable between his runners and, taking a deep breath, began to slide down, braking his speed as best he could with his feet. The cable seared his palms, but he ignored the pain. Then his feet hit the water. As they did so, the cable was whipped from his grasp. Now he was floundering, his injured hands stinging from the salt water.

A wave lifted him up and thrust him back towards the cliff. Instinctively he plunged forward, flattening himself. His feet struck the cliff face and he pushed against it with all his remaining strength. The momentum carried him forward, the backwash lifting him even further out. The next wave washed over him, and he found himself under the water. He couldn't breathe and panic gripped him. But he fought it.

He knew he was a competent swimmer. He was not going to die – not now. His head cleared water and he took a deep breath and began to swim towards the boat. The incoming waves fought him, but he had got away from the cliff face and had gained a little distance.

He struggled on despite the pain in his hands and the ache in his arms and leg. His sodden clothing didn't help, and seemed heavy as lead. On the crest of a wave, he glimpsed the boat making a tight circle. It was close. He was almost there.

He risked a backward glance. A man was climbing down the cable, already barely ten metres from the water. In seconds he would be swimming in pursuit.

Sean put more effort into his strokes, finding strength from somewhere. The boat came around, only metres away from him now. Jackie had opened the window beside the cockpit and he could see her clearly. He made one last desperate surge forward. He reached the boat as Jackie brought it around, holding it steady on the throttle.

But the boat rode the waves like a cork. The guard rail was too far above him to reach up and grasp it. The boat, lacking momentum and sideways on to the sea, swept towards him; he would be crushed beneath its keel. He heard the engines rev as Jackie opened the throttle. She must have realised the danger. The boat surged away, leaving him to the mercy of the waves and his pursuer.

The boat swung in a tight circle, coming round again towards him. But this time it passed inside him. It loomed above him like a great sea monster, almost close enough to touch. Its wash buoyed him up and thrust him further out. Aware of what Jackie was up to, he began to swim again.

On the third circle, the boat slowed, the engine note changing as Jackie throttled back. He stopped swimming and a wave swept him back towards the boat. It was still bobbing like a cork, but no longer threatened to sweep over him. Another wave took him up to the boat and, for once, luck was on his side. The boat rocked, and as it swung back towards him, the safety rail came within his reach.

His strength had all but gone. But above the noise of the engines and the roar of the water, he heard Jackie call out to him. She was leaning out of the cockpit window, her face fixed with a fierce determination.

He made a last despairing effort, reaching up with one hand to grab one of the stanchions of the safety rail. Somehow he held on despite the pain of his seared palm and the ache in his arm muscles. With his other hand he grabbed the bottom rail and with a last superhuman effort, hauled himself up. Moments later he was falling over the rail onto the solid deck.

Lying there, gasping for breath, he heard the engines rev. The deck beneath him tilted as the bow lifted under full throttle. He closed his eyes, wanting to lie there forever. But there was no time to lose. He had to summon help if Jackie hadn't already done so.

Feeling jubilant despite his fatigue and anxiety, he scrambled to his feet. He grabbed the railing and looked back. The island lay astern. He saw the tower with figures on the roof staring after them. Glancing down, he glimpsed a man's head bobbing in the water as he struggled to reach the cliff.

Sean let go of the rail and made his way through to where Jackie stood at the wheel. She turned and smiled. He reached out to touch her shoulder.

'You saved my life,' he said. 'Thanks.'

'It's OK,' she said. 'I felt you might be worth saving.' She smiled once more, then turned away to give her attention to the sea ahead.

'Have you contacted the mainland?' he asked. 'Is help on the way?'

She nodded. 'I got through to the coastguard eventually,' she said. 'They're sending help. But they can't contact the island. All communications have been cut. My mobile phone doesn't work either. I think lightning must have damaged the masts.'

'I don't think that's the problem on the island,' Sean said quietly. 'You see, I cut the cables to the communication dishes on the roof.'

Jackie stared questioningly at him.

'It's a long story,' he said. 'I'll tell you all about it later.'

She nodded and spun the wheel, bringing the boat onto a heading which would take them back to the mainland. Sean stared back at the island. Hawk and Quigly were almost certainly still trapped in the strongroom and now he had no means of getting the codes to Costello in time to save them. If it wasn't already too late.

The noise of an engine from the direction of Oldport interrupted his thoughts. He cocked his head and listened. It was the unmistakable sound of a helicopter. Was it Hawk's helicopter returning to the island?

Jackie stared at him. She knew what he was thinking. They had almost made it.

THIRTY-ONE

From the roof of the tower, Costello could only look on helplessly as Sean Gunne make his escape. Enraged and frustrated, he watched the boat head out to sea, leaving the lone pursuer struggling in its wake. He didn't care whether the man drowned or not. His sole interest lay in his own self-preservation.

He stared into a clearing sky, seeking the helicopter. But there was no sign of it yet. Even if it did appear, without radio contact he couldn't order the pilot to try and prevent the boat getting away. And where was the speedboat? Had it even put to sea yet?

But wasn't it too late anyway? Howley or Gunne were almost certainly alerting the authorities right now, if the Howley girl hadn't done so. Even if they couldn't operate the boat's radio, they would soon reach the mainland and raise the alarm. His worst nightmare – to be trapped on the island – had come true.

A sound reached Costello from the direction of Oldport: the

helicopter. It was like music to his ears and he stared skywards until he saw the machine like a dark speck against the blue sky. He watched until it became the size of a bird, then ran for the stairs to the dungeon, taking them two at a time.

He found Corridan attempting to cut through the strongroom door. They had already lost communication with Hawk, and Quigly, if he were still alive, had made no attempt to contact them. He could have tapped on the pipes if he'd wanted to and the built-in microphone would have picked it up. So perhaps he too was dead.

'They've got away,' Costello shouted at Corridan. 'But the chopper's here.'

'It's over, then,' Corridan said, pushing up his visor.

Costello nodded. 'Hawk's dead or dying,' he said. 'Our only hope now is to get away before the police arrive. The chopper will take us to the airport where the Learjet's waiting to fly us out.'

'Right,' Corridan said, turning off the oxyacetylene torch. 'It's time to go.'

The noise of the helicopter landing on the pad in the court-yard reached their ears. 'Come on,' Costello said. 'Let's go talk to the pilot.'

The pilot was climbing down from the machine as they both ran outside, the rotors still turning. They waited until he joined them, then they retreated to the soundproofed entry hall where it was possible to speak above the engine noise.

'There's a lot of activity on the quay at Oldport,' the pilot said. 'There are police cars and people milling about.'

'Then we don't have much time,' Costello said. 'You'll fly us out right away.'

'And Hawk?' The pilot stared at them.

'Dead,' Costello said.

'And the others?' the pilot asked.

Costello shrugged. 'It's every man for himself. Now, get ready to fly us out.'

The pilot nodded and strode out to his machine. Corridan and Costello hurried off to collect what they needed for a quick getaway.

+   +   +

As the boat headed out to sea, Sean quickly gave Jackie an account of what had happened over the past few days. As he spoke, she stared at him with growing disbelief.

'It's incredible,' she said. 'I can hardly–' She stopped and they both listened. Above the sound of the boat's engines, they could hear another noise. 'The helicopter,' Sean said, springing for the window. He watched the helicopter soar towards them. He was convinced that it would try and interfere with their getaway, but it flew on and dropped down into the castle courtyard.

It was then he realised that Costello could not communicate with the pilot since the aerial cables had been cut. But he could do so now. The helicopter could be back in minutes to drop Costello's men onto the boat and take it over.

They were still over six kilometres from the mainland. How could he save Jackie? Could he persuade her to take one of the inflatable dinghies and try to get away while he led them off? Or could he take the dinghy and let her escape in the boat? But they couldn't outrun a helicopter in either craft..

Jackie was at the wheel, the throttle fully open. The boat had powerful engines, but it wasn't built for speed. And to Sean, inexperienced as he was with boats, their progress seemed agonisingly slow.

He glanced back at the island, which seemed peaceful now,

and saw another threat. Around the point of the island came a speedboat, heading straight for them. It skimmed the tops of the waves, its prow seeming to point vertically into the sky.

Before he could call out a warning, the helicopter rose into the sky above the tower like a black bird. This was surely the end. Sean's stomach tied itself in knots.

He stepped away from the window. Jackie stared at him, her face reflecting his own fear. But there was a firm determination in her eyes. She didn't speak, but leaned across to the window and looked skywards so that she could keep the helicopter in view. She obviously intended to try and out-manoeuvre it if she could.

Sean felt a surge of pride. Jackie, like Liam, was one of the bravest and most resourceful people he had ever known. It would be a terrible thing if she were to die. At the thought, anger and rage engulfed him. Let them try and take over the boat – they wouldn't go down without a fight. Quickly he looked around, seeking a weapon with which to defend them.

'Sean?' Jackie's voice sounded urgent.

'Yes?' He swung towards her.

'Look.' She pointed skywards and he stepped back to the window and looked up. The helicopter was heading for the mainland. Sean watched the helicopter, thinking that it was just manoeuvring to come at them from a different angle. As it soared further away, he realised that it was not coming for them at all. But there was still the speedboat. He looked back to see that it had slowed. Then as he watched, it swung about and began to go back the way it had come.

'Costello's running,' he shouted triumphantly at Jackie. 'He knows it's over.'

'We've won,' Jackie said, her voice jubilant. 'Your father is safe now.'

'But not Hawk or Quigly,' Sean said. 'They're almost certainly still locked in the strongroom. They'll die soon, if they're not already dead. I can't leave them.'

'Hawk would leave you,' Jackie said. 'He would have us all killed.'

'Maybe,' Sean said. 'I just don't know anymore. But no matter what he's done, or might have done, I can't be responsible for his death. I have to go back, Jackie.'

'No,' she said. 'Leave that to the gardaí.'

'It'll be too late,' he said. 'They don't know the code to get them out. I do. Now that Costello has fled, there's no one else to save them. You have to turn back and drop me off. Then you can head for the mainland. It's their only hope.'

'No,' Jackie said. 'Let me radio the codes to the gardaí. They can let Hawk and Quigly out.' She stared at him defiantly, her jaw set.

Sean reached out and gripped her hand. 'It could be too late then, Jackie,' he said. 'I can reach the castle before the gardaí. Even a minute might mean the difference between life and death for Hawk and Quigly. I locked them in; if they die it will be my responsibility, and I couldn't live with that. How could I face my Dad or Liam again, knowing what I'd done?'

'When I locked them in the strongroom it was only so that I had something to bargain with. But my plan went wrong. Then, when you arrived on the scene I thought that once we'd got safely away, I could contact Costello on the boat radio and give him the code. I hadn't considered that I might have cut off all communications. So now I have to go back, Jackie. You understand that, don't you? I have to go back if I'm to live with myself.'

'But what if this Costello hasn't gone?' Jackie said, her voice near to breaking. 'Perhaps that was just the helicopter pilot making his getaway. And what about the other guards? It's too dangerous, Sean. You could still be killed.'

Sean shook his head. 'Costello's gone,' he said. 'Without a leader, the other guards will be too busy trying to save themselves. I'm Hawk and Quigly's only hope now. You have to turn back and drop me off.'

Jackie stared at him, biting her lip. Her anxiety was visible in her eyes and she seemed on the verge of tears. Then, with an angry shake of her head, she spun the wheel to bring the boat about.

'Pull in as close as you can, well beyond the end of the cliff,' Sean ordered as they drew close to the eastern shore. 'There,' he added, pointing. 'Where the rocks end. I'll swim ashore and climb up to the castle. It's a fairly steep climb, but it's the quickest way of reaching the castle right now. And radio the coastguard again. Tell them Costello's almost certainly heading for the airport. There's still time to stop him getting away.'

Jackie nodded, but didn't speak, and he knew she was upset. But this was something he had to do. He stood by as she skilfully manoeuvred the boat towards the shore, seeming to know by instinct how close she could safely get.

'Thanks, Jackie,' Sean said. 'I'll be all right. You head for Oldport as soon as I'm gone.'

'Good luck,' she said. 'And ... and do take care.' There was a break in her voice as she turned away.

He opened his mouth to speak, but stayed silent. Then he ran out onto the deck and dived into the sea, striking out for the shore. When he reached the safety of the beach and scrambled out of the water, he looked back. Already the boat was heading back out to sea and he felt abandoned. What if Jackie was right and Costello was still here? By the time help arrived, Costello might have taken his revenge.

Sean thrust these thoughts from his mind and began to

scramble up the steep slope, using heather and rock for hand and footholds. He seemed to have found new strength from somewhere and soon reached the top. Once there, he looked back. The boat was well out to sea now and he could see its wash like a giant comma drawn in the water. In the distance he saw another boat coming from the mainland. Help was on the way.

He turned and ran the two hundred or so metres to the castle. His wet clothing made running difficult but he pressed on. The gates stood wide open. There was no one to be seen, not even the dogs. Had everyone fled or was Costello still here, waiting for him? Sean hesitated, then realised there was only one way to find out. Taking a deep breath, he ran through the gates and the archway into the courtyard.

The doors to the tower stood open. There was no sign of life. When he entered the hall, the silence was eerie. There was an acrid smell of burning on the air.

He quickly made his way down to the dungeons. The gate on the stairs to the tower stood open, the metal charred and twisted from the heat. The strongroom door, the metal slightly charred, was still closed. Sean reached to key in the code but stopped, suddenly aware that he couldn't face what might await him inside.

He ran to the door of his father's room and punched in the code. 'Dolittle'. The door opened immediately. Denis Gunne's face registered disbelief and shock and joy. He hurried forward, his arms outstretched, and clasped Sean to him.

Sean drew away from the embrace and grabbed the lapels of his father's white coat. 'Help me, Dad,' he said urgently. 'I locked Hawk and Quigly in the strongroom. They might still be alive, but there isn't much time.'

'What do you mean?' Denis Gunne said. 'I don't understand.'

'I'll explain later,' Sean said. 'Now come on.' He grasped his father by the arm and dragged him with him.

At the door, fingers poised above the keypad, Sean hesitated. Then taking a deep breath, he punched in 'Wodehouse'. There was a hiss of compressed air. The door swung open. Vapour billowed out. Again Sean hesitated. What if Hawk and Quigly were already dead? He shivered, but it wasn't from the cold.

Instinctively he reached out to grasp his father's arm again, suddenly frightened of ghosts – of skeletal hands reaching for him, cold as the grave. He saw the glass coffin first, ice-encrusted, vapour partly shrouding it. He moved forward, still holding his father's arm. The air chilled his lungs as he breathed. No one could have survived, he thought. He would find Hawk and Quigly dead and he would have to live with their deaths for the rest of his life.

He moved around the coffin and saw the figures huddled in the corner. Quigly had taken Hawk from the chair and had wrapped his arms around him to try and keep him warm. They were both motionless and Sean gasped, gripping his father's arm tighter still.

Then Quigly slowly raised his head as if it were made of lead. His eyebrows were fringed with frost and his face was the colour of polished alabaster. Puffs of white vapour blew from his mouth as he gasped for breath. But below the eyebrows, his eyes still flickered dully.

Denis Gunne gently released Sean's grip on his arm and went forward. He dropped down on his haunches beside the two men and reached towards Hawk. His fingers probed beneath the collar of the padded jacket. Sean held his breath, knowing that he would relive this moment for the rest of his life.

'He's alive.' His father's voice was surprisingly calm and Sean knew that this was the professional medical doctor speaking.

'But we need to get warmth into his body immediately. Go to the nearest bathroom, Sean, and run a warm bath,' he ordered. 'If we're quick I think we have a chance to save him.'

As Sean left, he saw his father grasp Hawk beneath the armpits and begin to drag him out of the strongroom. Quigly was following on his hands and knees.

His mind in turmoil, Sean ran to the bathroom and began to fill the tub, testing the temperature with his fingertips as he did so. It was just ready when he heard footsteps approaching.

He turned to see Quigly enter. The man had Hawk, the outer padded suit now removed, cradled in his arms. Quigly looked even more ghostlike than before and Sean marvelled at his strength and determination and above all, his dedication to Hawk.

Denis Gunne followed and helped Quigly to lower Hawk into the warm water. Sean had his first glimpse of Hawk's face. It seemed waxen, with a sheen to it like plastic. His eyebrows were coated with ice, and his chest rose and fell rapidly as he struggled for air. Somewhere deep in his lungs, there was a rattling sound as if some creature struggled for life down there.

'Will … will he live?' Sean asked, frightened of the answer.

'It's touch and go,' his father said. 'It depends on how much he wants to go on living. If he's determined to live, he'll live. But if not …' He shook his head and turned on the hot tap. A steady stream of steaming water added its heat to the water already cooling in the bath. 'Massage his hand,' Denis Gunne ordered Quigly, and realising the man couldn't hear him, indicated what he wanted him to do. 'Sean,' he added. 'You take his other hand.'

Sean didn't want to touch that cold, waxy flesh. But he forced himself to walk around to the other side of the bath. Hawk lay in the steaming water, submerged almost to his neck.

He might be dead but for the puffs of vapour from his mouth and the heaving of his chest and that awful rattling in his lungs.

Taking a deep breath and summoning up all his courage, Sean reached down and raised Hawk's hand from the water. It was cold and heavy and lifeless. Sean suppressed a shiver. 'Leave it in the water,' his father said. 'We must keep it warm. Massage it there.'

Sean lowered the hand into the water, where it no longer felt so heavy, and began to rub it. He glanced across at Quigly who stared back impassively. Sean looked away and concentrated on what he was doing.

Time passed; it seemed to Sean like hours. Denis Gunne let out some of the water and turned the hot tap on again. Suddenly Hawk coughed and spluttered. Sean jerked as if stung and stared at him. Hawk's face twitched and his eyes half opened. On the other side of the bath, Quigly made a sound. Sean glanced up and stared at the man.

Quigly's face was as impassive as ever. The blue eyes still glinted coldly But twin rivulets of tears ran down Quigly's cheeks. The huge man was crying

THIRTY-TWO

It rained on the day Abraham Silvermann's body was flown back to Texas. Sean Gunne watched the report of the event on the television news bulletin that evening. There was film of the coffin being removed from the morgue. In the background, Hawk Silvermann sat in his powered wheelchair, a lonely figure hunched against the wind and rain. Quigly, who had recently been released from prison on bail, stood beside him, holding an open black umbrella.

Sean stood in his grandfather's kitchen and stared at the pictures, remembering a frozen boy in a glass box. That had been five weeks ago, but still the face of the dead boy haunted his dreams. Perhaps when Abraham Silvermann was eventually laid to rest, the dreams would no longer plague his sleep.

Sean listened to the voice over of the reporter covering the removal. 'It is Mr Silvermann's wish,' he heard, 'that his son's body be returned to Texas for burial. In a statement issued today, he makes it clear that he has come to the conclusion that it was wrong to want to have his dead son cloned. He no longer wants his son to be alone and so has arranged that the boy's body should be laid to rest with that of his mother.'

So Hawk had given up his dream to clone his son, Sean thought as he listened to the reporter. Did that mean that there would be no more stem cell research, no more attempts at curing his paralysis?

The reporter went on to give details of Sean's escape from Fair Island and what had happened since. 'Sergei Bukanov's body has already been returned to Chechnya and buried with his family,' he said. 'The security guards who worked on the island are in prison awaiting a decision on whether they are to be extradited to the US to stand trial for more serious crimes. Mr Silvermann will be now be returned to the secure psychiatric hospital where he is undergoing evaluation to see whether he is mentally competent to be tried for kidnapping and false imprisonment.'

As the news item ended, the telephone rang. Sean picked up

the kitchen extension. 'Hello,' he said.

'Sean?' It was Jackie. 'Did you see the news?'

'Yes. I was just watching it.'

'I thought it was so sad,' she said. 'Didn't you?'

'I suppose,' he said, not certain of how he had felt. Since his escape from Fair Island, his feelings had been all mixed up and Liam was constantly in his thoughts. Sometimes he found himself wondering if he had done the right thing in escaping from Fair Island and bringing an end to Hawk's dream. What if the research had come to fruition and Hawk had kept his word and used stem cells to cure Liam? What if? What if? He knew the question would torment him until the day he died.

'How is Liam?' Jackie's voice broke into his thoughts.

'He's fine,' Sean said. 'He's supposed to go on some new drug treatment next week. Dad seems to think it will slow down the progress of the disease. We'll just have to wait and see. Having Dad's name cleared of any wrongdoing has really helped him, I think.'

'Tell him I said hello,' Jackie said. 'I'll be back from Oldport on Sunday night. Maybe we could all meet up on Monday. Around lunchtime. Is that OK with you?'

'Sure,' he said, brightening up at the prospect. Both himself and Liam had missed Jackie since she'd gone on holiday to Oldport nearly two weeks ago.

They chatted for a few minutes and arranged to meet on Monday. When Sean hung up, he muted the television and continued his preparations for the tea which had been interrupted by the news item. His father would be back soon from his surgery.

Denis Gunne still lived here with his father and Sean often stayed over, but more and more found himself staying at home with Liam. Denis visited everyday. He and Beatrice were stiff and formal when they were all together, but the tension which had been present before was now absent. There was no more talk of divorce, at least for the moment, and sometimes Sean dared hope that the family might yet be reunited.

He heard the key turn in the lock of the front door. His father was back. Sean reached for the switch on the electric kettle and pressed it.

+   +   +

On Monday, Sean emerged from his grandfather's house and headed for the bus stop. He was looking forward to meeting Jackie and anxious not to be late. He didn't notice the black car parked at the kerb until he heard his name being called as he passed. He stopped, poised on the balls of his feet, ready to flee, still wary of strangers and sudden noises.

He turned to meet the gaze of a man in a chauffeur's cap. The man sat behind the wheel of a dark Mercedes. He smiled and Sean felt somewhat reassured. It was a summer's morning and there were people about. It was hardly likely that anything could happen to him here.

The darkened rear window of the Mercedes slid open to reveal Quigly. He stared at Sean, his face as impassive as always. He proffered Sean a white envelope. Sean took a step backwards and shook his head.

'I'd take it if I were you,' the chauffeur said. 'Otherwise he'll follow you until you do. It's from Mr Silvermann.'

'I don't want it,' Sean said.

'He'll follow you everywhere,' the chauffeur repeated. 'And I do mean everywhere. But it's your decision ...'

Quigly gestured that he should take the letter. Sean remained undecided. If he didn't take it, Quigly was likely to pursue him as the chauffeur had said. In the end he would be forced to take it just to get away from him. Sean stepped forward and took the letter. The window slid back up and the car drove off. Sean stood and watched until it turned right at the end of the street.

He turned his attention to the letter and noted his name handwritten on the envelope. Why would Hawk be writing to him? It didn't make sense. Intrigued, Sean opened the envelope and removed the single sheet of paper it contained. He read:

Dear Sean,

This is by way of an apology to you and your father and your family. I hope you can forgive me. I am slowly getting better, though I dread the future and what the consequences of my actions will be.

I want you to know that I loved my son, Abraham, more than life itself. I would have gladly given my own life for him. That is something I know you will understand.

I want to make recompense to you and your family. I think I can give all of you some fresh hope. Will you come and visit me so that I can tell you what I have in mind? I know it will be difficult for you, but despite everything, will you come?

I will send Quigly at noon tomorrow to bring you to me. If you do not come, I will send him every day this week. If you still do not come, I will know that you do not wish to see me and I will respect your decision.

Yours hopefully,

Max Silvermann.

Sean re-read the letter, folded it, and put it back in the envelope. He slipped it into his pocket and continued on his way. He did not speak of it to Jackie nor to anyone in his family.

The car arrived outside the house at noon the following day. It waited five minutes before driving off. It was there again on the next day. On Thursday, Sean was waiting on the pavement when the car pulled up. Quigly opened the rear door and Sean sat in. They drove off in silence.

+   +   +

'Thank you for coming,' Hawk said.

Sean nodded and took a seat across from Hawk who sat in his powered chair. The male attendant who had brought Sean to the room stood just inside the door, his arms folded.

The room contained just a hospital-style bed with a locker and the chair Sean sat on. The single window was tall and narrow and covered with a steel mesh. The only personal item in the room was the photograph of Abraham Silvermann which had stood on Hawk's desk, and now stood on the bedside locker.

'Why did you want to see me?' Sean asked, his voice cold.

'I want to make amends to you and your family,' Hawk said. 'And I want to create something lasting to commemorate my son's short life. But to accomplish both, I need your help.'

'What can I do?' a puzzled Sean asked.

'The most important thing of all,' Hawk said. 'And that is persuading your father to help me.'

Sean stared at Hawk in amazement. 'Help you? After all that you did to him, you–'

'I know,' Hawk interrupted. 'You think I'm crazy. Maybe I am. But let me explain what I have in mind. Then you can decide.'

'I am a rich man,' Hawk went on. 'I once believed that money could buy anything. Now I know that is not so. And even if money could buy anything, there are some things we must not buy. You understand?'

'I ... I think so,' Sean said.

Hawk nodded. 'Your father is a brilliant man. He is one of the finest geneticists in the world, but that talent is being wasted. Ironically, this has been caused by those, like myself, who saw money as their god. That is a great tragedy.'

'I know he helps people now. But any doctor could do that. What they cannot do is the research that your father is capable of. That sort of ability is a gift – from God if you want to believe in Him. But a gift nonetheless, as rare as sporting prowess or musical ability. I want to give your father the opportunity to use that gift and I want you to persuade him to accept.'

Sean shook his head. 'My father would never accept,' he said. 'And I would never try to persuade him. He gave all that up because he hated it.'

'No,' Hawk said emphatically. 'He didn't hate the research. He hated the greed and exploitation behind it. And perhaps the nature of the research too. But that wouldn't happen if he accepted my offer.'

'Why not?' Sean asked.

'Because he would be in charge,' Hawk said. He waited a moment to let the words sink in. 'I am willing to provide him with unlimited funds to build – in Ireland or wherever he wishes – the most modern research establishment in the world into stem cell technology. He can hire the best scientists and researchers in any area he wishes: biology, genetics, computers. He will be solely in charge and will decide every aspect of its operation. He will decide what's ethical or not. No one, not even myself, will interfere with his decisions. There will be only one condition ...' Hawk trailed off.

From outside came the noise of traffic. Sean was only now becoming aware of it. It was as if Hawk had stopped the world for a few minutes. But Sean was back in the real world again, facing the man who had brought so much fear and misery to himself and his family. He should have nothing but hatred for him, yet did not.

'It is not a major condition,' Hawk was saying. 'It concerns the name of the establishment. It will be called the Abraham Silvermann Research Institute. I want it to be a worthy monument to my son's memory. The only way I can ensure that is to have a man of genuine integrity in charge. That man is your father.'

+   +   +

The Mercedes dropped Sean at his grandfather's house. He was still reeling from his visit with Hawk, and his mind was in turmoil. 'It is up to you now,' Hawk had said. 'You're the only one who can persuade your father to accept my offer. You know it is the right thing to do. If his research is successful – and I know it will be – he will give hope to so many, including your brother.

'You must convince your father to visit me to discuss the matter. After that we must hope. I will send the car again each day next week. If your father doesn't come, then I'll know that you've failed.'

Sean got out of the Mercedes and it drove off. He didn't enter the house, but set off walking in the wake of the car. He was unaware of his surroundings until he reached the roundabout on the main road.

It was here he had come that morning his father disappeared. It was quiet then, in contrast to the continuous traffic that now roared by. So much had happened since then, and he knew that the world could never be the same again.

That morning he had been close to despair. Now, he felt the first stirrings of hope. Ironically, it was Hawk Silvermann, who had almost destroyed everything, who had given him that hope.

Sean turned and started to walk back. As he did so, he began to rehearse in his mind what he would say to his father when he told him of Hawk's offer. When he reached Orchard Road he went straight on, heading for his father's surgery. He was anxious to speak to him while the hope was still fresh in his mind and he still believed that dreams could come true.

Other Books from The O'Brien Press

OUT OF THE FLAMES
Vincent McDonnell

Maria's father sends her to Ireland for safety after her mother is murdered by the corrupt Malangan regime. She encounters hostility and suspicion, but also makes friends with David, a local boy. When the past catches up with Maria in the shape of Jonah Kegale of the secret police, David is the only one who can save her.

Paperback €6.95/STG£4.99

JUST JOSHUA
Jan Michael

Joshua is like any other village boy – helping at the market, making money from the tourists. But there are whispers about his father. Can he really be a 'mountain man' and what does this mean for Joshua's future?

Paperback €6.95/STG£4.99

THE HARVEST TIDE PROJECT
Oisín McGann

Taya and Lorkrin accidentally release a botanist working in captivity on the secret Harvest Tide Project, triggering a massive manhunt by the sinister Noranian empire. With the help of a barbarian mapmaker and their Uncle Emos, the two must stop the Noranians and the disaster the project was designed to create ...

Paperback €7.95/STG£5.99

BENNY AND OMAR
Eoin Colfer

For Benny, the family move to Africa is the end. Nobody plays his favourite sport, hurling, and school is weird. Then he meets Omar. A madcap friendship develops between the two, and their antics become the bane of village life. But real life intervenes and the boys must outwit the village guards, Benny's parents and, ultimately, the police.

Paperback €7.95/STG£5.99

BENNY AND BABE
Eoin Colfer

Benny is visiting his grandfather in the country for the summer holidays and finds that as a 'townie' he is the object of much teasing by the natives. Babe is a tomboy, given serious respect by everyone. Benny may be a wise guy, but Babe is at least three steps ahead of him – and he's on *her* territory. Babe runs a thriving business, rescuing the lost lures and flies of visiting fishermen and selling them at a tidy profit. She just *might* consider Benny as her business partner. But things become very complicated, and dangerous, when Furty Howlin wants a slice of the action too.

Paperback €7.95/STG£5.99

THE JOHNNY COFFIN DIARIES
John W Sexton

Johnny is a drummer in *The Dead Croco-diles*. He goes to a school with the biggest collection of Murphys in the country, where the teacher, Mr McCluskey, is trying to destroy his mind with English literature. He is also the reluctant boyfriend of Enya, an arm-wrestling champ with a man-eating pet. Life is very complicated for a twelve-year-old!

Paperback €6.95/STG£4.99

Send for our full-colour catalogue